- A SWEET PRIDE & PREJUDICE ROMANTIC COMEDY -

Mr. Darcy
STEALS
A KISS

(AND SOME OTHER STUFF)

ALIX JAMES

CONTENTS

Copyright		V
Dedication		VI
1.	One	1
2.	Two	7
3.	Three	14
4.	Four	21
5.	Five	29
6.	Six	37
7.	Seven	45
8.	Eight	56
9.	Nine	62
10.	Ten	69
11.	Eleven	81
12.	Twelve	92
13.	Thirteen	106
14.	Fourteen	118
15.	Fifteen	129
16.	Sixteen	137

17. Seventeen   149

18. Eighteen   158

19. Nineteen   166

20. Twenty   177

21. Twenty-One   187

22. Epilogue   199

23. From Alix   208

Also By Alix James   210

Also By Nicole Clarkston   212

Free Ebook from Nicole!   215

To the man who stole my heart.
Thanks for putting up with all my silliness.

ONE

Elizabeth

"**P**APA! NOT AGAIN!"

My father looked up from his worktable, his glass dropping from his eye. "Ah, there you are, my dear. Nearly finished. What do you think?"

I pushed aside the door to my father's hidden cottage and surveyed his latest creation—a vase about nine inches high with a crack at the mouth that ran down most of the side. It was painted in black with gold relief, portraying ancient-looking figures driving chariots or carrying swaths of wheat or entwined in scandalous embraces. "I think you ought to be in the house reading your books and balancing your ledgers, as Mama believes you are, rather than out here painting vases."

"Yes, yes, my child, and I will do, when I have cleaned the paint from my fingers. Just a touch more of the gold leaf... there. Now to thrash it about a little for proper effect, yes? Oh, I think it will do nicely in my study, and then after a year, we shall move it to the drawing room, and after that, who knows?"

I shook my head and cleared away his brushes and paint pots. "You'll never stop, will you?"

He chuckled and hung up his painting frock. "Of course not, my dear. What would be the sport of that?"

I tsked and sighed as I checked his shirt collar and sleeves for paint drops. "Sport, indeed. What shall you do when you are discovered?"

Papa slid his arms into his jacket. "Discovered! Nonsense. Why anyone should bother is beyond comprehension. I have done nothing but add a bit of beauty to the house."

"And the houses of about twenty others, all of whom think they purchased an artifact from antiquity?"

"And have they not? Who can tell the difference? Why, if there is a difference, it is that mine are better, and I challenge anyone to deny it."

"And what of our uncle, who brokered these transactions, thinking the pieces were genuine?"

Papa held the door of his cottage for me and locked it behind us after we were both outside. "But they were, my dear! I have not the pleasure of understanding you. A vase is a vase, is it not? It graces the mantel handsomely and improves the aesthetic of any house. I should think it would even hold flowers if anyone cared to defile it so. Why this obsession with where it came from?"

I closed my eyes and counted to three. "Oh, nevermind, Papa. Mama is calling for you through your library door, and she thinks you have gone deaf again. She is so convinced of it she means to send for Mr. Jones to examine your hearing."

"Well! I suppose I am in luck that she has not tested the lock, then. What seems to be the crisis this afternoon?"

"Oh! Nothing important. Something about Netherfield Park being let at last. I care little for it, but she is perfectly convinced it will be well-stocked with single gentlemen of large fortunes."

"Truly! Perhaps our new neighbors are fond of antique art."

"I dearly hope not."

Papa laughed and put his arm around my shoulders to pull me close and kiss my cheek, as he used to do when I was small. "My darling girl, my vases are not the only works of art I possess. If our new neighbor has any sense at all, he will be at my door within a fortnight, seeking to add a little beauty to his home."

"A request which you will naturally refuse until his fascination has grown into obsession, and he is willing to offer triple what he once thought an outrageous price."

"But of course. What do you take me for, an amateur?"

Darcy

I TUCKED MY MAGNIFYING glass into my coat pocket and straightened. "Magnificent. Truly, Uncle. I've not seen a more exemplary sample of Hellenistic sculpture in many years. The rearing stallion with the hero swathed in his battle raiment—absolutely remarkable. Hercules, is it?"

Lord Matlock shifted his pipe to the other side of his mouth and beamed. "I thought you would approve, Darcy. Lord Elgin was reluctant to part with it, but at last, I carried my way."

"Did you, now? You did not say you got it from Elgin. I imagine he demanded quite the price."

Matlock huffed. "Not as such. It's that former wife of his, bleeding him dry. Pockets to let, he is. He's moved his entire collection to what is little better than a coal-shed while the debt collectors chase him down. I say, 'tis is a wonder he can feed himself. When a man's purse is bankrupt, his principles soon follow."

I removed the handkerchief from my pocket to dust down the marble statue. Such a fine piece should be accorded all the dignity and reverence I could offer it. "I thought he intended to sell the entire collection to Parliament. A shame for it to be broken up. It is a national treasure, and not necessarily England's. Byron is fit to be tied over Elgin's plundering of Athens."

"Aye, and I would keep these statues safe if by any means I can. There is the 'collection proper,' as was, but you must have heard of the shipwreck just after it sailed from Greece. A whole boat full of art sunk to the bottom of the sea and 'mostly' recovered?"

I nodded gravely. "You think he has more than he claims?"

"I do. Naturally, in his diplomatic roles, he could have access to any number of 'gifts' such as this, as well as the right people kept silent. Lesser known pieces, ripe for scavengers to scrape up and scatter while Parliament deliberates and Elgin himself is starving."

"Indeed! How many has he let go? Sold off to the black market, I shouldn't wonder."

Matlock nodded and puffed on his pipe. "Word is he parted with two or three last year, but I cannot verify it. He was very cagey with me. Cannot have it widely known that the collection Parliament would buy is not complete, you know? That is why I sent for you."

I gave the sculpture one last admiring glance, then shot my cuffs and squared my shoulders. "Of course. My agent is connected to various networks, some of which are legal—certainly, you take my meaning."

Plumes rose from the pipe as my uncle walked behind his desk. "Yes, yes, I have the same connections. I've no need of runners and thugs. What I want is a fellow who can wander into drawing rooms and casually admire the decor. You're a bachelor in high demand; no doubt full up of invitations to just about every fine house in the country."

I lowered myself into the chair opposite Lord Matlock's grand desk. "What makes you think someone who had bought such a contraband masterpiece would display it?"

"Display it? Come, come, Darcy. They cannot help it. Everyone simply must have his Greeks and his Romans to adorn his house, and if they cannot find or afford an original, they have someone like Flaxman or Sergel create modern masterpieces after the old style. Some of them dashed convincing if a man did not know his sculptors. Most would not give it a second thought. But you've an eye for the right sort of thing, and that is what I am after."

"You are asking me to pretend to court a dozen noble daughters in whom I have no interest, merely to spot potential missing pieces of the Elgin collection, which are only rumored to exist." I shook my head and laughed. "Insupportable."

"Not a dozen. Not even five." Lord Matlock opened his drawer and withdrew a piece of paper. "Two, for the present."

I glanced at the paper. "Lady Catherine? Surely not!"

Matlock grunted. "My sister has an eye for quality and few scruples regarding where she obtains it. Fear not, for I have sent Richard to her. He can wander Rosings with greater impunity than you can. It would not do for your activities to arouse Lady Catherine's scrutiny."

I nodded, my stomach uncoiling in relief. "And the other? I do not recognize this name. Is he of the House of Commons?"

"Hardly! No, Bennet is a small holdings gentleman, barely of any account. But he was said to be a fair classic at Oxford. Educated in archeology and spent several years in Greece before his elder brother died, and he had to return to England to inherit. They say he was so put out over the affair that he married the most ridiculous woman he could find and produced only daughters, just to spite his dead ancestors."

"And he knows Elgin?"

"It is possible. All I truly know is that Bennet is rumored to sell pieces from his own collection rather frequently—one would say *too* frequently for a man of his means. Where does he get them all? And last year, he went to Scotland, close to where Elgin has his miserable abode, with his brother-in-law, a merchant named... there it is. Gardiner."

I stroked my thumbs together, contemplating what Lord Matlock was asking of me. "If my 'casual' perusal of this Bennet fellow's household results in raised expectations for one of his daughters, I place the blame on your head."

My uncle grinned around his pipe. "I've no fear. You've slipped many a noose already, Darcy."

Two

Elizabeth

"HIS NAME IS BINGLEY, and he comes from the North. They say he has a large fortune, and he is bringing a party with him of seven gentlemen and two... my dear, are you even listening to me?"

Papa raised his listening trumpet to his ear and squinted. "Oh, indeed, Mrs. Bennet. Seven ladies, and how many gentlemen did you say?"

"I did not say! Rather, you have got it quite backward. Oh, I do not know why I even bother! Jane, you heard me properly, did you not?"

Jane hid a smile. "Indeed, Mama. Seven ladies and two gentlemen."

"Far too many ladies," I added.

"Seven *gentlemen!* Can no one hear a word I say?" lamented Mama.

"It's this dratted paraffin in my ears," Papa said, too loudly for the size of the room. He twisted his listening trumpet as if screwing it into his ear. "There, that is better. What is this you say about Ringling?"

"*Bingley,*" Mama shouted at him. "B-I-N-G... Oh, what is the use? You will forget it the moment I say it."

"Would that I could, my dear, but tragically, I recall everything you tell me. Why, just the other day, you described to me the great excess of lace on Mrs. Purvis's daughter's friend's sister's wedding gown. After that, I had the pleasure of learning everything there never was to know about Lydia's newest embroidered handkerchief."

"My dear, you underestimate the importance of a well-embroidered handkerchief. It is a lady's first signal to her amour that she... Mr. Bennet! You are not listening again!"

"Quite so, Mrs. Bennet. And if you will excuse me, I intend to not listen from my library, where my chair is comfortably worn, and the walls do not shout at me."

I turned in my chair as Papa rose and scowled at him. The unrepentant rascal. He merely winked at me and then at Jane, who was giving him the same look.

"Mr. Bennet, you have no compassion on my poor nerves! I daresay when Mr. Bingley arrives in town, you will not even trouble yourself to greet him, and your own daughters will suffer for it."

"Far be it from me to let my girls suffer. If he is the sort of cad who cannot sniff out their beauty from Netherfield, I daresay he does not deserve them."

Jane and I exchanged glances. Papa could keep me laughing all day long, but his treatment of Mama was growing tiresome. He felt no shame for it, of course, and it was worse that I could hardly keep a straight face when he riled her up. But it truly troubled Jane.

"Oh!" Mama put her handkerchief to her breast and fluttered it as Papa left the room. "He *would* scamper off to his cursed library, and just when I was about to tell him the most important thing!"

"What is that, Mama?" Jane asked.

"Well! Mrs. Long had it from Lady Lucas, who got it from Mrs. Brown, who heard it from her housekeeper that there is a thief in Meryton!"

"A thief?" I asked mildly. "Oh, goodness me. There is always someone willing to pick the pockets of the careless."

"Nay, for this is no ordinary thief. They say he broke into Mrs. Marcus's larder and stole an entire ham, and then he took all her silver spoons."

"Spoons!" I ejaculated. "How is she to stir her tea?"

"Indeed, it is a hardship! And there is another report that he pinched a fine tapestry from Lady Trenton in Halstead and a necklace from Mrs. Howell in Raleigh."

"How do we know these are all the same person?"

"Oh, by his own actions, to be sure. He scarcely bothers to sneak in. Rather, I believe he hopes the lady of the house will catch him so he can rough her up a bit as he robs her blind!"

Jane stiffened. "Surely not!"

"And the worst of it," Mama continued, "is that he is apparently so charming that the lady declines to put up the hue and cry. Lady Trenton reportedly swooned when he left her. She was that overcome."

A smile tugged at my mouth. "So, you are saying there is a scoundrel going about kissing ladies in their own homes and cozening their finer possessions before they have quite come to their senses? I believe I should like to see a man of such talents."

"Lizzy, you do test my nerves so! As bad as your father you are, but you will see this is no laughing matter when he accosts someone you know. I'll not have him slipping into *my* house and compromising *my* daughters, I'll not. I'll have Hill sleep in the drawing room if need be. Heaven knows I cannot depend on your father to hear an intruder before he causes mischief."

Jane looked at me and sighed, shaking her head. I pointed up subtly, and she nodded. We'd have a long chat upstairs.

Darcy

"A MR. CHARLES BINGLEY to see you, sir."

"Bingley? There's a surprise. Send him in, please." I flicked closed the pages of the peerage book I had been leafing through. This Mr. Bennet of Longbourn had a strange family history, but it could wait. I stood to button my jacket.

Charles Bingley, two years my junior and son of a woolen mill tycoon, was an old acquaintance from Cambridge. We had never been close, owing to the rather significant gulf between our stations and social circles. However, I had always found him an amiable chap with no faults of character or taste. He had a tousled mop of fiery red hair and the freckles to match, but he had the good sense to pair them with such a genial aspect that none could object to his less-than-dignified appearance.

He entered the study wearing a smile as wide as my desk and put his hand out. "Darcy! Thank you for seeing me."

"Of course. Won't you sit down? Tea?"

"Yes, thank you. I hope not to take too much of your time. I shan't wish to impose."

"Not at all. Dobbs, will you ring for tea? And close the door, please. What can I do for you, Bingley?"

"Well, it is probably quite silly. Actually, I am not certain I ought to have troubled you at all, but as I was in the neighborhood—"

I gestured. "Please."

He released the breath he was holding. "Very kind. Well, as you recall, my father sold the mills several years ago and had intended to purchase an estate upon his retirement, but he got the itch to travel instead. The golden Orient, the Coliseum in Rome, the Pyramids at Giza; he quite wore out his boots."

"Indeed? I did not know. Where is he now?"

"Northampton. In the family vault."

I was reaching for a tin of fine cigars to offer him, and I froze. "I am sorry. I did not hear."

"'Twas about a year ago." He shook his head when I offered the cigars, and I put them away. "He had got so far as Turkey when he died, and they sent him home in a box. But I am being rather morbid. I am sorry, Darcy."

"Quite all right. My condolences. How can I be of help? I take it you mean to carry out his wishes and purchase an estate?"

"Purchase? Not at all. No, no, far too much bother. But I should like to try it for a time, as he was persuaded that owning an estate was the pinnacle of all life's charms. I have recently taken the lease on a fine property, not half a day's drive from London."

"Well, congratulations."

"Thank you. We've nearly all the details sorted, and I am to take up residence in a fortnight, but there is the bother of the house's furnishings."

I tilted my head and crossed my arms. "The furnishings? Ah, here is Dobbs."

We paused our conversation as the butler held the door, and a maid pushed in the tea tray. Bingley took more cream and sugar than tea in his cup while I had mine served nearly black with no sugar. He stirred his tooth-decaying froth as I took the first sips of my proper tea and leaned back in my chair.

"I am afraid I know little of furnishings—chairs and tables and what-not," I said. "I suppose they are all shabby, and the landowner is exacting tuppence for wear and tear during your lease? What you want is a broker. I am happy to give you a name."

"No, no, it is not the chairs and tables. The house holds a fair bit of fine art."

"Does it? Well, perhaps I can be of help, after all."

"I hoped you might. The landowner is retrenching and selling whatever he can that is not owned by the estate and destined for its heirs. The rest, he is valuing at far above what they are likely worth, in case something is broken."

"Indeed. Troublesome, but not altogether a rare tactic."

"Yes, and I was hoping to seek a second opinion on certain items. There is also some confusion in identifying one or two pieces, as no one seems to be able to find out where they came from. I believe the owner wishes to sell them, but he cannot prove they do not belong to the estate. One record says one thing, while someone else presents a contrary statement as to both their origin and their worth."

"And you would like me to help you settle any disputes? I am happy to."

Bingley's smile grew wider. "Capital! There is just one problem. I cannot have it known that I am bringing in my own adviser—not just yet, anyway. I fear it might give unnecessary offense, and if nothing is truly found amiss, I would not wish to muddy the waters, so to speak."

"I quite understand. How would you wish me to proceed?"

Bingley toyed with his teacup. "You could come merely as my guest. We say you have come to enjoy the autumn shooting. Hurst, my brother-in-law, is coming, and I've invited Soames and Watterson. It would not look odd, I do not think."

I clucked my tongue. "That depends on how careful you wish to be. To anyone who cares about such things, I have something of a reputation as an expert in fine art."

"Oh, yes, indeed. That will not do at all. And if there is anything to know, I ought to know it before I move my slippers in." He sighed. "Well, what if I get you into the house on the sly, perhaps, before I am to take up residence?"

"Quite possible. Where is this estate of yours?"

"Hertfordshire, about four miles from the town of Meryton."

I blinked and set my cup aside. "Meryton? As it happens, I have business there anyway. When did you wish to leave?"

Bingley's face glowed. "As soon as possible. Tomorrow?"

I narrowed my eyes in thought. "Tomorrow. Yes. That will do."

THREE

Elizabeth

"JANE, WE MUST DO something about Papa. His little hobby is becoming a terrible risk." I was pacing a circuit around my bed, snatching swallows of my tea or nibbles of my biscuit each time I passed by the tray.

My eldest sister, seated at the foot of her own bed, sipped daintily at her cup. "Oh, yes. Poor Mama. He does delight in teasing her so."

"I was not thinking principally of Mama, but yes. His pretense of deafness is a perfect nuisance, and he is utterly incorrigible. However, I was speaking of his vases. I caught him painting another one today."

"Oh, dear. How long do you think before he manages to sell this one?"

"Who knows? A month? A year? I am more concerned with 'to whom' and 'for how much.' One day, he will sell one of his 'ancient artifacts' to someone who will have it examined, and I fear the higher the price he demands, the sooner that will happen."

Jane nodded thoughtfully, cradling her teacup in one hand. "But he is only amusing himself by selling vases to his friends for ten or twenty pounds. 'Tis a large sum for many, but to the sort of people buying his vases, it is but a day's entertainment. Surely, once they have admired it a little, they put it on a shelf and forget all about it."

"And what happens when Uncle Gardiner gets a touch too enthusiastic about one piece or another and promotes it to the wrong person? Many there are in London who could uncover Papa's forgery and blast our family's reputation. Only think of it! If one is found out, the rest will surely follow until nothing is safe from scrutiny. No respectable man would ally himself with one of us after that. And think of Uncle Gardiner!"

Jane drew a long sigh. "It would be the worst of all things. No one cares if a gentleman defrauds the poor. They become terribly indignant if a man of lower station should swindle the rich. There could be no forgiveness."

"Forgiveness! One has to survive to be forgiven, and I am certain we could not. But the trouble is, I am almost beginning to believe Papa wants to get caught."

"Why in heaven's name would he want such a thing?"

"For sport, what else? Because he has got big-headed with how many people he has hoodwinked, and he thinks his talents are a match for any expert."

Jane shrugged. "Are they? Papa spent years studying ancient ruins. He probably knows what they look like better than any man in England."

"That is just what he would like to think, but I tell you, there are men who make it their object in life to know more than he does. And it is not just the vases. Last week I found him with that sculpture on his desk, and he was writing a letter to someone about it."

"Sculpture?" Jane repeated, her voice heavy. "You don't mean..."

"The only valuable sculpture we have. The one of Eros and Psyche where they are..."

"Please! I know what they're doing. But what was Papa doing?"

I shook my head. "I do not know, but Jane, I've a terrible feeling about it. As he was scrawling out his thoughts, I heard him mutter 'His Highness'."

"He wouldn't! No!" Jane looked horrified, then laughed. "I am sure you must be mistaken, Lizzy. Why would His Royal Highness receive a letter from our father? It is beyond imagination."

"Unless Papa claims to have brought something back from Greece during his travels that no one else has. It doesn't even need to be addressed to the Prince Regent. He will learn of it soon enough if Papa directed his letter to someone of high enough rank. Have you not heard the tittle-tattle or read the broadsheets? There is considerable interest in gathering the classical sculptures out of the hands of private collectors and placing them in the keeping of the Kingdom."

Jane fell silent. "Well, what of it? If Papa can sell it—"

"He will bring more attention to his collection of vases."

My sister paled. "Oh, dear. Truly?"

"Positively. And who is to say the sculpture itself can withstand scrutiny?"

"You do not think it's a forgery? Impossible! Papa never learned to carve marble. He only dabbles in pottery."

"I don't know. It might be genuine, it might not be, but I doubt Papa cares about the truth in any case."

"So, what do we do?"

I finally stopped pacing and dropped onto my bed. "I have tried for years to make him stop. Since I was old enough to know what he was doing in that hidden woodsman's cottage of his. Nothing has worked so far."

"Well... what if we were to tell Uncle Gardiner?"

"Oh, Jane, never! Poor Uncle could not live with himself if he ever found out. Oh, it is terrible of me, but I would not do that to his conscience. Surely we can think of some way to stop Papa without tormenting our uncle."

Jane set aside her cup and pulled a pillow into her lap. "Well, Lizzy, you're the clever one. You'll have to think of something, or we may all be ruined."

Darcy

"WHAT A... CHARMING TOWN." I took my walking stick from the carriage and turned about, surveying all that fell before my eye. There was a smallish town square with brick pavers, though the streets surrounding them dissolved into packed dirt. The paths were lined with various street hawkers, a speckling of red-coated militia officers, a two-story inn—hardly worth calling an inn—and two or three modest shops with children's handprints all over the windows.

Bingley stepped out beside me, fisting his hands at his waist. "Is it not? I was quite taken with it. Netherfield is just a bit farther on. Shall we take a luncheon and hire some saddle horses to ride over this afternoon?"

I cast another glance about, then turned back to Bingley. "Indeed. Have you met any of the neighbors?"

"Scarcely anybody. My agent lives here and has told me all about the town, but I have not been introduced to anyone else."

"That may be in our favor for now."

We stepped into the inn and walked to the tap to speak for two rooms. The innkeeper himself greeted us with a wide grin. "Ah, Mr. Bingley! We are pleased to see you again. Come back to make all your preparations, eh?"

I slid a glance at Bingley, and he flushed crimson. "Well, I mean *almost* no one." He offered a nervous chuckle. "Ah, Templeton, there's a good man. Look, I'd just as soon everyone did not hear I was passing through today. We've still contracts to sign, that sort of thing. Wouldn't want anyone to get the wrong idea about my visit, you understand."

The landlord winked and pointed. "I understand, sir. I'll put you down as Mr.... Scarlet. Two rooms? Private dining room to refresh yourselves?"

Bingley's mouth twitched, and I hid a smirk. He had always been a touch sensitive about his hair. "Er... thank you. Yes. Shall we?"

I PEERED THROUGH THE hedges at the house. Bingley had been so unnerved by the notion that the landlord would hear of his visit before the house was officially his that he brought me round the back way, avoiding the primary drive. It was a fine enough structure, stately yet pleasingly modern, but one thing struck me.

"Did you not say you were to take up residence in a fortnight?"

"Yes, if all the conditions are satisfactory."

I stood in the irons to get a better view through the hedge. "Where is everyone? People should be stocking the larders, filling the coal-shed and the wood-sheds, bringing hay for the stables."

Bingley blinked. "Oh. Well, yes, of course. I am sure they are about somewhere."

I sat down in the saddle. "You have not ordered the house to be prepared?"

"Well, it is only that I thought perhaps I ought to wait until all my questions were answered. It should only take a day—two at most to see everything done, should it not?"

I pinched the bridge of my nose. "Have you at least interviewed a housekeeper?"

"Oh, as to that, there is one in residence. She should have a letter from me by now to retain the cooks and maids she will require."

"You are keeping on the old master's housekeeper?"

"Is that not fitting? I thought as she knows the house and the people she might employ... I would not wish to turn someone of experience out on her ear."

"Unless her loyalties cannot be depended on."

"Oh, dear. Well, how shall I proceed?"

I shook my head. "For now, let us take stock of these items in question. We can speak of staffing the house later. I presume your housekeeper will let us in?"

"I do not think..." Bingley squirmed in his saddle. "That is, I had nearly forgot."

I swung about to stare at him. "Forgot what?"

He cleared his throat. "I just recalled that I had a letter back from her, and she is in Plymouth at the moment, visiting her daughter. She was not to return until Friday."

"You forgot. How does a man forget such a thing?"

"Well, ahem. You know how it is, Darcy. Quite a deal going on, of course. Hard to keep it all straight."

"Yes. That is why I write things down." I sighed and swept my gaze over what I could see of the house. "Well, we have come all this way. Surely you have a key."

"Not yet."

"Not... Exactly how did you mean to get into the house?"

He gave me a weak grin. "Oh! I am sure a dust boy or milk maid would—"

"Except you have not hired them yet. And as I look round and see no livestock and a garden that has been let grow wild, I doubt you shall find anyone."

Bingley crumpled his mouth and worried his reins between gloved hands. "Well, old chap, I am afraid I have wasted your time. Unless... you do not think we could slip the latch on one of the windows, do you?"

I sighed. "I am ashamed to confess it, but yes. I know how to do that."

Four

Elizabeth

"**W**HAT NEWS DO YOU bring us, Sister?"

I was standing in the hall when a flurry of lace and ruffles flounced by me so quickly I could hardly have recognized their wearer. But I did not need to. Mama never moved faster than when someone was at the door.

My Aunt Philips had come to call, and she was still putting off her hat and gloves at the door when Mama fairly grasped her by the shoulders and shook her from head to toe. Uncle Philips stood by, calmly glancing about for Hill to take his hat.

"Oh, you will never guess it. It is the most delicious of all things!" Aunt gushed. "Come, take me to the parlor and send for tea, for I have so much to say."

Mama squealed in delight, and they hooked arms to run off and tell their tales. Uncle gave me a thin smile. "Afternoon, Elizabeth. Jane. Is your father about?"

Jane and I traded glances. Papa had *better* be about. "Let me look into his study for you," Jane offered.

"You appear very grave, Uncle. Something important?" I asked.

"Just business, Lizzy. I've a duty to see all my responsibilities attended to with dignity and precision."

I folded my hands. "Yes, of course. Shall I have Mrs. Hill bring a tray?"

"No, thank you. If your father is at his liberty, I will ask him to accompany me on an errand."

Jane emerged from Papa's study just then, behind Uncle Philips' back, and our eyes met. She gave a subtle shake of her head. I groaned. Papa was probably at his kiln again.

"I am sorry, Uncle," I said. "Perhaps he has gone to call on Sir William. Is there something we can do to help?"

"Oh, I should think not, no. I only wanted his advice on some matters at the Netherfield property."

"I did not know you had any involvement there. Are you Mr. Rumfield's agent?"

"No." He tugged at the lapel of his coat and squared his shoulders. "I have been retained by Mr. Bingley to look after his interests in the transaction. I should like first to be certain the house is secure after the reports we have heard of a housebreaker."

"Oh, it is true, then!" Jane said. "We heard something of him."

"Quite true, I am afraid. He has carried off a small fortune already. I daren't think what might happen if he should come to Netherfield while the house is empty, and the housekeeper is away."

"Surely there is no fear of that. According to Mama," I put in with a chuckle, "he only ransacks houses where a lady is present to work his wiles upon."

"All hearsay, Lizzy. Nevertheless, I think it best if I take an additional account of the present valuables. I wanted your father's opinion on Rumfield's collection of... are you sure he is not in? I saw his horse grazing in the field."

Jane paled, and her eyes grew large. "He is ill," I blurted.

"Ill? I spoke to him yesterday, and he was in excellent spirits."

"Well, you know how stomach ailments can come on all at once like that. One minute, he is eating all the buttered scones, and the next... But, of course, I needn't elaborate. I am sure he will be feeling much better by tomorrow."

Uncle Philips frowned. "More's the pity, for I was to send Mr. Bingley my letter by today. I suppose I shall have to make do without his help. I say, though." He pursed his lips, tilted his head, and scrutinized me. "Did not your father train you in his arts?"

I laughed. "Arts! Whatever are you talking of? Papa has no artistic pastimes. Indeed! Only think of it, Jane. Papa wielding a brush! Why, 'twould more likely be used for a bookmark than dipping paint."

Jane laughed nervously. "The very idea!"

"No, no," Uncle said with an impatient wave of his hand. "I did not mean the creative sort of art. The man is brilliant at evaluating rare and costly collections, and he told me you had the same interests and an enviable eye."

"Well, I don't know about that, but what did you need, exactly?"

"I want someone who can tell me what is what, and I depended upon your father to help put down the value of certain articles at the estate. It is not only the rumors of theft troubling me. I had a letter from Mr. Bingley last week that Rumfield is being a bit of a bother over the affair, and I would not like to lose my fee merely because no one knows the worth or origin of some silly old vase."

Jane clapped a hand to her mouth and stared at me. She was shaking her head and gesturing wildly with her free hand.

"You know," I said slowly, my eyes still on Jane, "I do believe I could be of some help. Papa taught me all about such things. I would be happy to try, at any rate."

"Excellent! I will wait by the carriage while you collect your wrap."

Uncle Philips went out, and Jane rushed to my side to clasp me by the arm. "Lizzy, what are you doing? You know nothing about real art!"

"I know enough about the fake stuff! Don't you realize those items in dispute are probably ones Papa made? I would rather give our uncle something that will satisfy him than force him to look elsewhere for advice. Only think if he feels it necessary to bring in a proper expert?"

"Indeed, that could be very awkward."

"Keep Mama distracted while I am out. And if Papa should return smelling of paint or with pottery dust on his shoes, hide him away until I am back!"

"You can count on me, Lizzy."

Darcy

"J UST A LITTLE LOWER... a little lower..."

"Is that it?" Bingley called. He was dangling by his fingertips from the leaded glass window overhanging the second-floor library shelves, his toes brushing the tops of the wood.

"You are quite safe. Only do not throw yourself from the window like..."

Too late. Bingley gave a swing of his legs and skidded off the top of the shelf, banging every protruding surface from the front of his body on the ledge on his way down. His fall was accompanied by such a rapid succession of thuds and smacks that none could say how many bruises he would number by the time he reached the bottom.

"Bingley!" I rushed to his side. "Are you quite all right?"

He rolled over, one hand clutching at his middle and the other holding his nose, which was already running red. "I think I have broken... myself." He fished for his pocket handkerchief to stem the flow. "This is quite a to-do!"

"Good heavens, you have done yourself a mischief. Come, we must get you up and away before you stain the rugs. No good sneaking in if you leave a trail of blood in your path."

Bingley groaned and permitted me to help him up. "I would to heaven there was another window! I do not fancy climbing back up that bookcase."

"We shall use the door when we leave. Here, take my handkerchief. Yours is already soaked through."

Bingley blinked and pressed the new handkerchief over the spoiled one. "The door. Of course. Pity that was the only window we could find access to. By the by, how did you learn to do that? It was devilish clever."

I gritted my teeth and ushered him more quickly down the stairs before his wounded nose could leak out all over the floors. "In my youth, I had a companion of questionable morals and a father who did little to impress upon me the unsuitability of following in his ways after my mother's death. I learned many things I ought not to have. Bingley, the bleeding is not about to stop. Take my second handkerchief. I fear we must get you out of the house at once."

"Yesh, I dink so. But how shall you carry on? You cannot know wish items to eggsamine." He squinted, then pinched his nose harder.

"I am far less concerned with the art in the house than with your condition. Make haste, for the handkerchiefs are nearly spent."

We were down the stairs now, passing by a grand entertainment hall on our left and a drawing room on our right. Bingley, for whatever foolish reason had inspired this bloody adventure, stopped dead and refused to move forward.

"Nere it is," he said through his blocked nose. "In ne drawing room." He tilted his head back, as if that would stop the bleeding faster, but it only made him sputter. I pushed his head forward again.

"There what is?"

"Ne collecshon of vases. Four alnogever, and... egad. Do you suppose by nose is bwoken?"

"Better your nose than your skull. Come away."

"I can fine by way out. Will you have a look at dem? Only for a moment to gib your opinion, den we snall be on our way."

"I could tell almost nothing in a moment. I would need to look at them in proper light with my glass to tell you anything of meaning."

"All I want to know is where dey came fwom and what dey might be worf. One minute, Dawcy? Den I will buy you an eggsellent dinner at de inn an we will be on the road back to London in de morning."

I sighed. "Very well. Meet me round the back with the horses. You say there are four vases?"

"Yes, about twelf inches high. Vewy old—do be caweful with dem."

"Of course." I waited till Bingley had seen himself safely out and was no longer in sight. Dripping blood on the front steps of the house could prove nearly as awkward as the upstairs sitting room.

"Now, then," I muttered to myself. "Where were these vases?"

Apparently, the housekeeper had at least begun to do her work because the furnishings were in various stages of cleaning. The drapes that would normally protect them from dust were mostly removed in the drawing room, at least. The room held a fair collection of paintings and so on. None too rare or costly, but respectable, nonetheless. The paintings seemed to have been selected and hung in their places based on the color scheme rather than any great depth of taste or understanding. I scanned the room lightly and found the set of vases I sought gracing the mantel.

They were very much in the classical style of Amphora pottery, with a narrow foot, a voluptuous body, and a slim gullet, graced with twin handles in the shapes of feathers or braids or simple round columns. Each was a burnished clay tone with Attic black detail and edging that resembled the Parthenon or animal processions or other such glories. The central figures included athletes, chariot horses, Dionysius at the grain harvest, and warriors with their swords. One even appeared to be Hercules battling the Hydra. The detail was exquisite. Altogether, they were a striking collection.

Gently, I lifted the nearest from its perch to inspect it. Sixth century, I should think. The artistic peculiarities of the era were all in place. Minimal evidence of restoration, though I could clearly see one place where a crack had been mended. To be expected for something of this age. It added to the value if the repair was nearly as old as the vase. The paint near the handle was worn, as many were. I scratched it lightly with my thumbnail and found the ancient paint was smoother than it appeared to be. That was interesting.

I picked up a second piece and was instantly struck by its weight. It was finely balanced, to be sure, but heavier than my memory informed me it ought to be. Curious! But then, it had been some years since I had studied Amphora pottery. My memory could have been imperfect.

I was reaching for a third vase when I heard the front door of the house open. Surely, that was Bingley, admitted at last by someone who kept the grounds. I heard a man speaking in the hall.

"This way, Lizzy. I believe the vases are in the drawing room."

My hand froze on the vase, and my lungs desisted from their employment. That was not Bingley, but two strangers, and they were coming to examine the very things in my hand. And I looked like a thief.

I cast about for some inspiration. I could simply confront them. I was doing nothing wrong. Well... hardly. It did look rather suspect. And Bingley had wished to keep his curiosity to himself until he had reasons to say something, so my presence could prove problematic for him.

A lady's voice echoed in the hall now. Botheration! I had no wish to terrify a lady! I could slip into the next room, but there was no time. The footsteps in the hall were coming closer by the heartbeat.

Not knowing what else to do, I ducked behind the fireplace screen, tucked my knees to my chest, and waited for them to leave.

FIVE

Elizabeth

"WHAT DO YOU MAKE of them?" my uncle asked. "Are they worth writing up in the lease paperwork?"

The vases were, without a doubt, my father's handiwork. Useful for decorating, like all the other replicas that graced fine homes. But Papa's vases did not look like replicas, and they had fooled some of the best "experts" in London—a significant source of delight for him. Certainly, he did not sell them for "replica" prices.

If it should be discovered later where Rumfield acquired them, and they were fake artifacts, it would be disastrous. Our only hope was that no one thought about them too much, or looked at them too closely. My mouth was dry, but I tried to formulate the most educated-sounding answer I could. My voice wobbled. "I am sure Papa would advise you to do so. They are very... ahem... very old."

"Are they? I've no eye for such things."

"Oh, indeed, uncle." I was a terrible liar. I hated doing it, and I never did, save when I was trying to keep my father from disgracing himself. I raised the nearest vase and tried to force my fingers to stop trembling.

"You see this one here. It is an image of the ancient god of wine and merriment. Quite a common motif of the fifth or sixth century, Papa tells me. I should think this vase alone would be worth..." I thought quickly. "T-twenty pounds."

"Well, that is not so bad. I feared something on the order of several hundred, from the look of it."

"But I am no expert," I answered jerkily. "Everything depends on its condition, of course. It could be worth many hundreds to the right collector. I am certain Uncle Gardiner could give his opinion if you wanted it."

Uncle Philips pursed his lips. "No, that will do, Lizzy. No one is trying to sell these artifacts. I only want to know how they ought to be managed for the lease. If you say they are worth noting, that is satisfactory for me. I will make the necessary amendments."

I let go the breath that was threatening to make me dizzy. I had averted the crisis. No one was profiting from my falsehood, and no one ought to lose by it. I was merely representing Rumfield's property as he no doubt believed it to be, and this Bingley person could pack them away for safekeeping if he had rowdy children who might break them.

"Only one more thing," Uncle Philips said. "I was to look in on a painting upstairs and verify that it is still here. Rumfield claims he left it, but it was not noted before. Care to come with me?"

"I am afraid I know nothing of paintings, Uncle."

"Very well. A pity your father was not available, but I can manage this. I'll not be a moment. Then I can drive you home."

My father. An image of him hearing of our visit to Netherfield and setting out himself to join us danced through my mind with all the allure of a blackening thundercloud. I could not have *that*. If I could not hasten my uncle away, perhaps I could meet my father on the road and turn him back. "Oh, but is that not very much out of your way?"

I asked quickly. "I can happily walk back to Longbourn. It is barely three miles."

"My dear Lizzy! Surely your mother would not hear of it. No, no. I brought you, and I shall deliver you home safely."

"Thank you, Uncle, but I must insist. I always take my constitutional in the afternoon, and the weather today is very fine. It will save me the trouble of setting out again once I have got home. Truly, I will have it no other way."

"Well... if you insist, Lizzy. I think it frightfully dangerous for you to wander so far, what with the reports of thieves and miscreants about. Has your father never forbidden it?"

"No, never, so long as I take care to bring none of them home."

He rolled his eyes. "Very well. Off you go, now. I will set out when I have done."

I watched him go, a tremendous anxiety easing from my chest. All would be right. I was that relieved, truly, so much so that I was swaying where I stood. I put a trembling hand out behind me to rest it on the fireplace screen. It was flimsier than I thought and shifted beneath my weight.

But that was not what startled me. It was the soft grunt of a body behind the grate that sent my poor heart into apoplexy.

Darcy

T HE YOUNG LADY WAS a fair athlete, I had to confess. An instant after she kicked the fire screen into my ribs, she had scampered across the room with one of the vases in her left hand. Her right clutched a silver candelabra, which was even now poised threateningly above her head.

"Who are you?" she demanded. "Show yourself!"

I had been only peering over the screen, instinctively holding my ribs, but what I saw of her eased my concerns. Why, she was but a girl! Or, rather, a young lady, but possessed of an intelligent face and lithe figure. Certainly, no shrew or farmer's wife who could set up an alarm or deliver a roundhouse punch to my jaw. I pushed the screen aside so I might stand.

"Stay back!" she cried.

From the corner of my vision, I caught her right hand lifting that candelabra, and then I was flat on my back, nearly slain by that great lump of silver hurtling at my temple. She'd thrown the thing with brutal accuracy, and it was a moment before I could see anything at all.

I was still behind the screen, though it was pushed out considerably from where it had been. My head was going to split apart where I lay. I was quite sure of it.

"Good God," I moaned, gingerly touching the back of my skull. It was sticky and wet where it had met with the fireplace bricks upon my landing. "What the bloody devil are you about, woman?"

Her disembodied voice wafted over the screen. "Oh! What a relief. I thought for a moment you were dead."

"I might be. Come, tell me if this is merely blood leaking out of me or if you have knocked a hole in my brain."

"I will come no closer! Who are you, and what are you doing here?"

I parted my hair with weak fingers, feeling for the gaping hole in my cranium I was sure must be there. All I found was a deep gash and a considerable deal of pain. Curse it all, Bingley had both my handkerchiefs! I had nothing to stanch the flow, which was even now spreading on the bricks and into my coat.

Gingerly, I pressed at the knot on my head and sat up. The world shifted and spun, but then steadied around the young lady's face. "Lizzy," the man had called her. A daughter of Longbourn.

Whatever in the world she was doing there, she sounded like precisely the person I needed to talk to. But how to explain my presence to her? I had technically broken into the house! I could not risk my good name by revealing myself to a gentleman's daughter.

I held up my free hand in a placating gesture. "Fear not, madam. I mean you no harm."

"You are the thief!" she cried. "The one everyone has been making such a fuss about! Stay where you are, or so help me, I will knock out more than your brains." She shifted the vase to her right hand and reared it back with clear intent.

Her words spurred inspiration. She was prepared to believe I was a known housebreaker? Very well, I would become one for the moment, if only to save face for us both. "I suggest you reconsider," I answered mildly, trying my best to recapture my dignity. It was not easy, with blood pouring from a throbbing wound just behind my ear.

"Why? To give you time to trick me? I am no simpering fool!"

"I can see that." I carefully dusted the front of my jacket with my free hand. Fortunately, the fireplace had been properly cleaned, and I was not entirely covered in soot, but I would be lucky if my valet did not give his notice upon seeing my suit. "That vase is quite valuable, I understand. 'Twould be a pity if you were to waste it on my poor crown."

She blinked and lowered her weapon, and I did not miss the shifting of her dark eyes as she glanced about for something less dear to lob at me. "What do you propose I do, sir? Pretend I did not just catch you in the act of plundering valuables?"

"That would be the simplest solution, indeed. One might then ask what you were doing here as well, since I take it this is not your house any more than it is mine."

Her jaw tightened, highlighting her rather fetching cheekbones. Not a conventional beauty, but quite interesting to look at when she was angry. "I am here on business."

"As am I." I stepped away from the screen.

She resumed her guard; the vase cocked near her shoulder, but I doubted she had the commitment to actually throw it this time. "I do not think I can credit your 'business.'"

"Be that as it may, a man must eat. Here, now, set that vase down before you drop it. Come, come, the way you are trembling, it will slip through your fingers. Look, here is a fire poker. Would you rather point it at me instead?"

Her eyes narrowed, and her chest rose and fell inside her bodice. Fetching, indeed. I forced my gaze back to her face, but it needed all my resolve. Slowly, she set the vase on an end table. "My uncle is within the house. All I need do is scream."

"I should think not, for you have already done so, and he has yet to charge in to your rescue. But fear not, for I mean you no harm. Only let me look at that vase there…"

She stiffened. "You are remorseless, sir."

"I am a man of duty, madam. I have a task to complete. That there will set me up most handsomely when I sell it in London."

Her eyes darted from the vase she had just set down to the others lining the mantel. "Sell it where? The illegal market?"

"Now, then, you do not think a man who dresses as I do would trifle with anyone but the best, do you? Wealthy collectors would pay a mint for something like this, legally obtained or not."

Her throat bobbed. "You cannot have the audacity to steal it still, after I have seen your face! And I do not think you are the sort to resort to murder to cover your tracks, or we would not be having this conversation."

"You are very clever, Miss..."

The lady lifted her chin. "Bennet. Elizabeth Bennet. And you are?"

"Oh, naturally, I have a name, but I cannot give it. You may simply call me... William. Yes, that will do. So, what shall we do about this little problem? For as you say, you have seen my face. Do you mean to turn me in for the crime of trying to steal the vases, Miss Bennet?"

Those expressive eyes flicked once more over the arrangement on the mantel. "I ought to."

"But you will not, for you have been alone in a room with a stranger, and that could prove problematic for you."

"Not just any stranger!" she shot back hotly. "A known scoundrel, a thief who steals precious items and then compromises ladies on his way out the door! Your reputation has preceded you, sir."

What the devil was she talking about? But best to play along, the sooner I might make my escape. "Indeed! I suppose it has. And..." I picked my way closer to her, enjoying how her spine stiffened, and she stood taller with every inch I gained. "What sort of 'compromises' am I accused of?"

Her mouth moved. "Why, I do not... it is not decent, sir."

I raised a brow. "Really? I beg your pardon, but I think the reports have been exaggerated. I would never dishonor a lady."

"Even as you rob her blind, you would not kiss her until she swooned senseless? I have heard all about you!"

"A clever tactic," I mused. "One that has its merits indeed. Suppose I leave the vases where I found them. Would that suit?"

Miss Bennet's shoulders relaxed a fraction. "It is the honorable thing to do."

"Oh, honor, fiddlesticks. What I want is far more important at the moment. How are you with a needle and thread, Miss Bennet?"

She tilted her head. "Lamentable."

"That is a pity, but I suppose you will still have to do. For I cannot very well see a surgeon about my predicament. No! Not after I was injured in another man's house, and as you were the one who threw the candelabra…"

"What precisely are you asking, sir?"

"Why, I should think it was quite obvious." I pulled my hand away from the back of my head to show it to her. "I am bleeding, and it is your fault. Therefore, I am asking you to stitch up the gash you made in my head."

Her lips formed a perfect "O," and her eyes widened. I was only just in time to catch her as she fainted dead away.

SIX

Elizabeth

"**B**LOODY BULLOCKS! WHERE THE devil did you learn to darn?"

I gave another remorseless stab of my needle into his flesh. "You ought to be grateful it is not my younger sister trying to piece your scalp back together. You would forever have a crooked seam under your hair."

"I am more worried about having hair at all! Must you be so violent? You have nearly—gah! Confound it, woman! That hurts!"

I broke the thread with savage glee and tied a knot against his head. Hard. "You ought to have chosen an honorable profession instead of skulking about houses and splitting your head open. I do not pity you, sir."

"A man has to make his living some way or another. I expect if I were a soldier, you w—in the name of all that is holy! Have you no mercy, woman?"

"You have a great gash here. Do you want your natural pate to slip off your head when they hang you?"

He raised a quaking hand to smooth over the uninjured part of his head. "Proceed," he replied through gritted teeth. "Only I do not know why you take such delight in tormenting me. What harm have I done to y—" He broke off with a hiss and an oath as I tied another knot.

"You came to harm my neighbor." I examined my needle and swapped out the remaining silk thread for another length. "Is that not reason enough for me to despise you?"

"Poppycock. He would not have been harmed in the slightest. I happen to know this for a fact." He turned his head to look at me as he uttered this last sentence, but I spun his head back around. Not gently.

"Thieves always say that when asked to justify themselves, I am sure. Another has more, so they think it right to take what does not belong to them. Well, you are quite wrong, sir."

He growled and hissed again, his teeth grinding against a foul assault of metaphors. When his eyes opened, there were tears of pain at the corners, and I almost felt an ounce of pity for him. Almost. "How is stealing from a man any different from deceiving him?"

I thought for a moment. "It is not," I decided as I pierced him again.

"And you have never been guilty of deceit? Disguise?" His face crumpled, and he snarled in pain as I tied off the last knot.

"Not willingly, which is more than I can say for the likes of you. There, I suppose you will still look dashing when they take you up before the Assizes."

"You think I look dashing?"

I gave him a dirty look. "You probably think you do." I set down the needle and sighed as I inspected my fingers, crusted with blood. And to my surprise, the thief's hand captured mine. His touch was... well, rather nice, though he was a scoundrel.

"Let us find you some water," he said gently.

My spine went rigid. "I think I would rather have nothing more to do with you, sir. I can find water well enough on my own."

"But you have done me a great service, and now I must see you right. Come, there must be a bucket over the kitchen hearth."

"That is not likely, as the housekeeper has been away for three days. I shall have to look to the well."

"And take the chance of stumbling on the groundskeeper? That might be an awkward conversation, Miss Bennet."

I scowled at him. "You really do have a troubling way of forcing me to consider propriety when it bothers you not a whit."

"Well, you have more to lose than I do, I am sure. Now, which way to the kitchen? Ah, here it is." He had yet to turn loose of my hand, a situation I found all the more unsettling because I rather liked the feel of his. Perhaps I really was a hoyden.

I cast a glance over my shoulder as we passed a row of windows and saw with a mixture of panic and relief that Uncle Philips' carriage had gone. He would know nothing of this little episode, and the story of someone trying to steal Papa's vases would not come to an investigation that could have ruined us. But I was now fully at the mercy of this strange thief.

"Aha! Just as I hoped. There is a little water left, no doubt what remained of her water for tea just before she departed. I say, this is something of a shoddy housekeeper, is she not?"

"I would not know," I answered primly, trying to retain something of my dignity. It was too late, for he had taken the bucket from the hook and set it on a worktable. Then he reached once more for my hands and plunged them under the water, scrubbing them with his own.

Good heavens, but this was scandalous, especially with the way he carefully caressed each finger, massaged the grooves between them, and stroked his thumbs into the centers of my palms. I could not draw breath, which was just as well, for the arrangement had me neatly tucked against his side, one of his arms draped casually over my waist, and my face nearly pressed into his shoulder. Breathing was no longer an option.

"There," he declared at last. "We are somewhat more decent now, are we not?"

"Sp..." I swallowed. "S-speak for yourself. I do not know how I will show my face in public again!"

"Nothing to it. You simply walk, do you see? Head high, shoulders erect, that's the idea. Your face will naturally accompany you."

"You are perfectly contemptible, sir! Do you not understand the trouble you have caused?"

"Trouble? How can there be any trouble if I stole nothing? Come, Miss Bennet, perhaps you ought to sit down for a moment before you go. You are looking fearfully pale."

"Perhaps it is because I have been frightened out of my wits, then manipulated into sewing up a stranger's head!"

"But I am not a stranger. I told you, you may call me William, and you are Miss Elizabeth Bennet. Tell me, should I call you Miss Bennet, or Miss Elizabeth? Are you the eldest sister out of the bunch?"

I narrowed my eyes. "What makes you think I have more than one sister?"

He turned away to hang the bucket, but for an instant, I thought his face registered surprise. "Oh! Merely an assumption. 'Twould be monstrous unfair of your mother to only pass on such beauty once or twice."

"You pay your compliments far too smoothly for my liking, sir."

"Do I?" He turned back and made a neat little bow. "You may be the first lady ever to say that to me. I am usually rather tongue-tied among the fairer sex."

"I doubt that! No, sir, you are a bounder. A rogue and a rascal and a liar, as well."

He pursed his lips and wandered closer to me, his eyes scanning me from head to foot. "You may be surprised to discover that I despise dishonesty."

"Yes," I retorted sarcastically. "That would surprise me very much."

"Very well. I see you do not believe me. I suppose there is nothing for it but to prove to you the honesty of my intentions. Shall I see you home, Miss Elizabeth?"

"Absolutely not!"

"But surely, it is not safe. I heard you say there is a housebreaker at large, and you know, you may encounter anyone on the road."

I stared. "You really are unbelievable."

"I cannot help what you believe, but I would not like any harm to befall you after you have been with me. I have my reputation to think of, you know."

I snorted and moved off. "I will take my chances. You, sir, ought to be grateful that I did not summon my uncle when you were a bleeding, sopping mess."

He caught up to me, a grin tugging at one side of his mouth, and he touched my arm. "I am sure I must be indebted to you for your kindness, then. One last thing."

"I want no more of your pithy remarks, sir. I—"

And that was all I got out, for in the next instant, I found myself gathered in his arms. He was gentle but firm, and I could not have resisted even if the thought had come to me. Which, lamentably, it did not.

Not even when he cupped my chin, stroked my cheek with his thumb, and kissed me until my knees turned to water, and I could not remember what day of the week it was.

Darcy

"**B**Y THUNDER, I THOUGHT you had got lost!" Bingley cried when I popped round the corner of the hedge. He was sitting in the most relaxed manner possible, slouching in the saddle, with his boots dangling beside the irons. He was still dabbing at his nose with what remained of the knot of handkerchiefs—a spoiled, bloody mess by this time. "Did you have any trouble?"

I caught the reins of my horse and leaped aboard without touching the irons. My body was positively humming, and I would need a good stiff gallop to get the tingle out of my limbs. Elizabeth Bennet... it was a name I would not soon forget.

"No trouble," I replied lightly. My first lie.

"You did not see anyone, did you? I thought I saw a carriage turning round the bend of the driveway, but it might have only been a drayage cart. Some farmer or worker, no doubt."

"No doubt," I echoed as I pulled on the rein. "Come, let us away before that can no longer be said."

Bingley scrambled to find the irons with his feet and move his horse off. "But the vases! Did you find them?"

"Easily."

"Well?" He was hunting the front of his jacket for the pocket, trying to decide where to stuff the ruined handkerchiefs. He finally settled for shoving it under the pommel of his saddle. "Should I be troubled about them or not?"

"In what way?"

"Are they worth what Rumfield's agent says? Is there any way of finding out where they might have come from? Who has the rights to them?"

"They are very fine," I admitted slowly. "I cannot say how long they have been Rumfield's property, but they appear to be everything he claims."

"Well, that's capital! Perhaps his word can be trusted about them, after all. So, are we off now?"

"Hmm. Oh, yes, indeed." I nudged my horse into a swift trot, but I wasn't thinking about the vases. My mind was back with that saucy snip of a girl who had bashed me in the head.

"Egad! Darcy, you are bleeding!"

Bingley had fallen just behind me, and now he raced to catch me up. He was pointing, aghast, as he surveyed the blood still splattered on the collar of my shirt and the matted hair that showed beneath my hat. "Good heavens! Did you have to come through that horrible window after all? I shouldn't wonder if you were knocked out. I ought to have come to look for you!"

My spine prickled, and I felt the tender back of my head once more. "Only a trifling bother. I am still in one piece, but your housekeeper may find a souvenir of my injury. I am afraid I... became rather involved in my examination and thumped my head on the hearth when I stood up again."

Bingley was regarding me strangely. "Well. We are a fine pair, are we not, Darcy? Here I was, thinking you would have nothing more to do with my clumsy self after this little adventure, but I see your luck is something like mine. Always getting into scrapes, as my sister Louisa says."

So, today was no fluke; he really was accident-prone. That was worrisome, because I liked this affable, unaffected fellow. But if he couldn't go anywhere without making a hash of things, it boded ill for him. "Speaking of scrapes, you will have a rather smashing bruise on your nose by tomorrow. I can see it already."

He winced and touched the tip of that swollen organ. "I am not eager to meet my new neighbors in such a state. Hopefully, it will be mostly healed in the next fortnight."

"Indeed. Do you know anything about the locals?" I asked casually.

"Only that my agent claims the county is full of beautiful young ladies. He promised to introduce me as soon as I have settled. Oh, I do wish you would come, Darcy. I had a letter before I left that Soames had begged off, and I fear Waterson may do the same, but it is a terrible pity. I hear the shooting is the best in the whole south of England."

Surely, a stretch of the imagination, but as I scanned the landscape, I could just fancy that the region held its charms. And not all of them were of the sporting nature. "Perhaps. I will speak with my steward, for I had intended to return to Pemberley for the autumn."

"Did you not say you had some business here in Hertfordshire, anyway? You could settle it when you come to stay."

"No," I replied, after a pensive sigh. "I ought to conclude that immediately. I think I will stay another night or two at Meryton. Perhaps when I return to London, I will have more answers for you regarding your vases."

"What answers? According to you, there is nothing irregular."

I blinked. "Oh, yes. Only a matter of curiosity, that is all." A great deal of curiosity. Fortunately, I knew where to find the answers.

SEVEN

Elizabeth

J ANE MET ME AT the door. "Oh! I feared you would be gone forever. Are you well? You look terribly shaken. Did you *walk* all the way from Netherfield?"

"Yes." I pulled off my gloves and pelisse and hurried to put them away. Oh, but my hands were trembling! I extended them, and my fingers quaked uncontrollably.

"Lizzy? Are you all right?"

I clenched two fists and forced a few deep breaths. "I will be. Come, Jane, we must speak with Papa. Is he in his study?"

She whirled into step behind me. "Yes, and he said he was attending to some very important correspondence and was not to be disturbed."

"Papa never has important correspondence," I scoffed. "But what I have to tell him is dreadfully important. Papa?" I pounded on his study door. "May I come in?"

"Lizzy!" Jane grabbed my arm. "There is blood on your sleeve? Are you hurt?"

I turned my elbow over to inspect my sleeve with a detached sort of curiosity. "It is not *my* blood. It belonged to the gentleman. How careless of him to mislay it."

Jane's brow dimpled. "Which gentleman? Uncle Philips?"

"Uncle Philips is not a burglar who bashes his head against fireplaces while trying to hide, now, is he? Papa! I must speak with you!"

"A burgl... a bur..." Jane's eyes crossed, and her head became suddenly wobbly.

"Not you, too!" I looped my arm through hers and swatted her cheeks to revive her. "I have had my fill of stitching broken crowns for one day. Papa!"

I raised my fist to pound on his door again, but it opened before me. I was scarcely in time to withdraw my hand before I popped my father in the nose. He was smiling, pleased with himself about something. "I am sorry, Lizzy. I thought it was Mrs. Bennet, come to tell me my tea is burning. Now, then, where is the fire, precisely?"

I marched into the study, dragging my woozy sister behind me. "Papa, there is a burglar in the neighborhood!"

He chuckled and closed the door. "Ah, yes. Your mother was telling me something of this. I hear he made off with an entire case of silver spoons! My, my, what have we come to? We shall all be reduced to stirring our tea with a butter knife."

"It is no laughing matter, Papa! I caught him at Netherfield—or, rather, perhaps, he caught me." I put a hand to my cheek, recalling how gentle his touch had been. The pleasant scents of sandalwood and pine still lingered, perhaps more in my imagination than upon my person. And his lips, warm and teasing and... and enough to make me feverish in places I never knew I had.

"Indeed, so you have seen this nefarious brute in person? Well, well, your mother swears he ravishes ladies for sport, but you appear unharmed. He did not molest you in any way, I suppose?"

I swallowed, and I was certain my cheeks were red as fire. "Not... much."

My father's bushy eyebrows raised, and for once, his smile faded. "You are serious, then. What happened? Are you well, my child?"

"I am well," I insisted, my voice a little stronger now. "Uncle Philips was in the house, after all. No harm came to me."

Papa drew a breath, a little paler than he had been a moment before. "That is well. Perhaps I ought to have heeded your mother's cautions a little better, eh? So, there really is some troublemaker going about ransacking houses? Did you speak to him? Who is he?"

"He said I might call him 'William.' Truly, I think he would harm no one, even if he is a bit... forward. But Papa, this is quite serious. You are in a very grave position, indeed."

My father strolled around his desk, stroking his chin. "Serious, you say. How so? If he means no harm to people and is only after a bit of property, I suppose the constable can manage well enough. I shall have Hill look round to the village for a few stout lads to guard the house until the trouble is gone. Unless, of course, he was handsome. In which case, I daresay no amount of guarding will keep Lydia safe from this rogue. Eh?" He chuckled and lowered himself into his chair.

"It is not that. It is *what* he was stealing that is the problem. Do you not recall the four vases Mr. Rumfield begged you to part with a few years ago? He was here nearly every other day, admiring first one, then the other, and he would not be satisfied until you had agreed to sell him all four."

Papa bridged his fingers on his stomach and laughed. "How could I forget? It was a bit of brilliance if I do say so. I hoped to offload only one, but in refusing to sell any of them, I persuaded him he could not be happy unless he had all four. He could have chartered a ship to the Mediterranean to find his own artifacts for what he paid for those!"

"And that is just the trouble, Papa. Mr. Rumfield paid a vast sum for forgeries!"

Papa waved a hand. "Pish-posh. They are exquisite samples of their type, and he was proud to own them. I wonder that he did not take them to Bath when he removed. Ah! Well, he probably did not have the space. I understand he is living in quite reduced circumstances for the present. Perhaps he ought to sell them, but I doubt not that he intends to return in a year or two. Cannot come home to a bare house, of course."

"Papa…" I kneaded my eyes and cut a sigh. "Please, one topic at a time."

"But of course, my dear! Forgive me. Now, tell me everything as it happened. And do sit down before you fall. Honestly, you look as if you might topple over if a strong wind were to come through."

Jane dragged a chair a little closer. Even so, I almost missed. Good heavens, what was wrong with me? I was still shaking like a leaf. It was that wretched man, the one with the dimple on his cheek and the… ah… deliciously tousled dark hair. That smelled like fresh air and saddle leather.

I gripped the armrests of the chair and blinked several times, trying to rid my memory of his charm and paint him as a proper rogue. "I went with Uncle Philips to inspect Mr. Rumfield's property because I feared he would be looking at the vases. As it happens, I was correct."

"Did he admire them?" Papa asked, that little wrinkle at the side of his mouth that betrayed his true interest.

"Yes, yes, of course, but pray, do not interrupt because I will lose track of where I was. I am afraid I led my uncle to believe they were quite valuable. I thought I was doing right, but now I worry that I have caused more trouble. What if Mr. Rumfield wishes to sell them, as you suggested? Why, then they would have to be appraised all over again, and this time, by a genuine expert."

"Indeed." Papa nodded, then shrugged. "Have you so little faith, my child?"

"I believe *you* have a great deal too much," I shot back. "Uncle Philips is trying to turn over what proof he can of where Mr. Rumfield acquired them, and you may be assured that if there is some scandal when they are found to be fakes, it will come round to you."

"Come, come, I am not worried. But you were trying to tell me about this thief. When did you encounter him?"

I put my fingers to my temples to massage away the beginnings of a headache. "It was when Uncle Philips went upstairs to look at a painting. I caught the man hiding in the fireplace, and I threw a candelabra at him."

"Hah! Good show, Lizzy! I expect he is very much knocked about, then?"

"Not nearly so much as he deserves. You ought to have heard him! Such a prideful, presumptuous fellow! I daresay he was not sorry at all for his profession and only wants another opportunity to plunder and thieve again."

Papa's brow crumpled, and he leaned forward. "So, he took the vases?"

"Hmm? Oh! No, of course not. He was too courteous for that once I had caught him."

Papa shifted in his seat. "You struck him with a candelabra and then had a long discussion with him?"

"Well, we had to stitch up his head wound. He was bleeding all over the carpet, and you know, Netherfield has those very fine Persian r—"

"You stitched his head!"

"It was easier than darning the rips in Lydia's stockings, but for the fact that he would not hold still. For someone who makes his living by burgling houses, he was quite the milksop."

Papa was blinking, his mouth hanging open. He shook his head as if waking from a reverie. "Er... yes, of course. What did this roguish milksop look like?"

I did not even have to think about that to recall every detail clearly. "Exceedingly tall with broad shoulders. Cultured way of speaking. Dark brown hair that curls just a bit, brown eyes with little gold flecks, a dimple in his left cheek and another on his chin. Very well dressed. Oh, and an imperious manner. He really was hateful, Papa."

Papa nodded, his eyes narrowing. "Yes," he breathed. "He sounds like a regular devil."

Darcy

"ARE YOU QUITE CERTAIN you will be all right? You must have taken a fearful blow to the head."

I dabbed a cloth to the back of my head to finish drying my hair. I had got the worst of the damage cleaned up, but without my valet, it was a dashed, inconvenient job. "I will manage. It is bruised and quite tender, but nothing more than I deserve for my carelessness."

"Yes. We are two of a kind, it seems. Louisa is forever teasing me that I cannot go anywhere but that I come home with some injury."

I raised a brow. "This is not a common experience for me. I was merely taken aback by... something." I touched the tender place at the back of my head again. That bewitching creature had left an impression, and not only upon my poor skull. When had I ever presumed such liberties? Never! And yet, I had been so free in speaking with her, in asking for her help... and in "thanking" her. I was still dizzy from that. What the devil had come over me?

"Perhaps I ought to stay, Darcy. I could be of some help, could I not?"

"I am afraid not at present. There can be no point in you remaining in Meryton when your business in London is not yet complete. My business will be concluded swiftly, and I will follow you tomorrow or the next day."

He looked unhappy. "Very well. How shall I thank you for all your trouble? I had hoped to invite you back to Netherfield when I am settled."

"Allow me to conclude my other affairs, and I will consider it. You are most kind to extend the invitation." I put out my hand, and Bingley took it with his face glowing with pleasure.

"Jolly good! Until we meet again, Darcy." Bingley replaced his hat, which did little to draw attention from the smashing black eye and swollen nose he had cultivated, and went out.

From my window, I watched him board the carriage for London. We had brought his carriage, which meant I would have to hire a horse or ride post for my return. That was as well. It was probably better if the Darcy carriage and crest were not seen anywhere near Meryton at present.

L ONGBOURN WAS A SMALLER estate than I had expected. Judging by the size of the house, the property likely brought about two thousand a year in rents—but that was just a guess. I arrived through the wood, not wishing to alert anyone to my presence just yet. How best to approach Mr. Bennet?

I could simply present myself at his doorstep, but I personally loathe such ostentatiousness. I cannot abide someone being so forward when we have not been previously introduced. Perhaps I could find someone in town to introduce me. That solicitor fellow…

Wait.

I backed the hired horse a little deeper into the trees when the front door of the house opened. Three young ladies, attired in varying shades of pink and blue, were wandering out the door. One was excessively high-spirited. I squinted… no. That was not the lady of my previous acquaintance. Too tall and round. The lady I had met was petite. Not voluptuous, perhaps, but her figure had a pleasing quality. Very pleasing.

I watched the others carefully. One was average in every way, and she walked with her arms clutched about her middle as if she despised being there. No, that was not my girl.

I snorted. *My girl.* What a silly way to think of her! I'd met the lady once. But she was clever and sportive, and it was no punishment to speak with her. She just might be the answer to my dilemma if I could spot her. Perhaps that third sister… No. The curls under her bonnet were frizzy and blonde, not rich, velvety brown with gentle spirals.

Ah, there. The door opened again, and two more young ladies appeared. One was a goddess. The other was another blonde. I smiled.

Even from a distance, Elizabeth Bennet caught and held my eye. Like a genuine diamond stands out from paste jewelry, like a well-bred filly rises above a plow horse. She might not have done, had I not already met her, seen her in all her scintillating glory. Others might even be drawn to that other sister, the second blonde who walked at her side. But they had not seen the mischief and the fire that I had seen, and I could not erase it from my mind's eye.

I backed my horse a little more when the ladies all stopped. They were walking on the road toward Meryton, but Elizabeth Bennet was hanging back from the rest. There was some discourse—the boisterous one was eager to go on and demanded that her sisters all follow. I held my breath to hear better. They were all supposed to stay together, the one sister said. Thieves afoot, she said.

But Elizabeth held her ground. Four would be enough for protection in town. She had something pressing to do at home. The debate lasted another minute, then the company parted. Four sisters walked ahead while Elizabeth turned back.

This was my opportunity.

I urged the horse forward to catch her before she reached the house, but she did not continue to her door. Rather, she watched over her shoulder for about ten paces until the others had rounded the hedge, and then she ducked into the woods to my right. Curious!

I slipped out of the saddle and hooked the rein on a tree limb. It would be easier to catch up with her on foot if she was making her way through the trees. I only wished to speak with her, to ask her some frank questions. She was a reasonable woman, or so she seemed. I cut through the brush and found a slight trail, little more than the path made by a deer.

But Elizabeth Bennet had vanished. One moment, she was there in front of me, her green pelisse nearly blending with the woods. The next...

I was seeing stars and sitting on my face, my posterior pointing toward the sky.

"How dare you follow me? Get up! What is the meaning of this?"

I groaned. Had she clubbed me with a whole tree? I spat out bark chips and tried to get my arms under myself, but she kicked me in the breeches. Not hard, but hard enough to topple me to my side, where I lay, shielding my face from the branch she shook over my head.

"I might have expected you to come back! What are you after this time? My mother's China? My father's books?"

"A word, madam. That is all. For pity's sake, stop hitting me with things! Do you often make new acquaintances this way?"

Her shoulders drew back, but she lowered her weapon. Then, upon glancing at it, she threw it into the thicket. "Very well. What do you want?"

Slowly, cautiously, I got to my knees, then my feet. "You are sure you are through injuring me?"

One slim brow arched. "That depends. I thought burglars were used to risk and injury. Part of the job description."

"Only if they're clumsy. Miss Bennet, I mean you no harm. I should think our previous encounter would be enough proof of that."

Her lips curved, and I found my eyes helplessly fixed on them. The softness of them, and the memory of how they had melted to mine...

"Our previous encounter taught me you are an opportunist and have no qualms about taking advantage of my good nature. So, what happened? Did one of your stitches come out? Trying to break into another house, I shouldn't wonder."

"Perhaps I ought to apologize. I did not intend to take advantage of you. I was... as surprised at myself as you were, no doubt."

"Oh, no doubt." She crossed her arms. "I hear that every day from men who kiss me without warning. How often do you use that pathetic line?"

"Only once, and apparently, not convincingly. Allow me to prove my sincerity, Miss Bennet. I come in peace, and I only want to ask you a couple of questions. I promise you, I will keep my distance, for I have no wish to add to my list of bruises."

Some eloquence sparked in those brown eyes of hers. Her thoughts flashed quickly across her face, from doubt to curiosity and finally to acquiescence. "Very well. What are you so desperate to know that you had to accost me in the woods by myself? You know you have the most deplorable manners, do you not?"

"And what of yours? You have nearly brained me twice this day."

"That is different. You are an enormous man, and I am but a defenseless female."

"Miss Bennet, you are many things, but defenseless is not one of them. Look, I am sorry for frightening you again, but it is important, and I could think of no simpler way to learn what I must know. Will you tell me, if you please, about your father's artwork?"

Her eye twitched, and for an instant, I thought she was going to reach for her club again. But then, she did something that shocked me even more.

She kissed me.

EIGHT

Elizabeth

IT IS SAID THAT a clever person ought to learn or do something new each day. I am often too willful and obstinate to heed such wise advice, but occasionally, I see its merits. For example, only last week, I learned how to create an exquisitely complicated embroidery knot, which I am certain will come in terribly handy if I ever need to use my handkerchief as a boat anchor.

Today, I learned that a man, even a frightfully stubborn and irritating man, can be distracted from just about anything when one kisses him.

But one must take care to do the job thoroughly. It is no good to go to the bother of kissing a man, only to have him resume his troublesome line of questioning in the next breath. No, to achieve my purpose, I needed him senseless and drooling—just a step or two above comatose. And so, I released his lapels, which I had twisted into my fists to pull him down to my level, and plunged my fingers into his hair.

He had very nice hair.

And nice hands. I know because they had found their way around my waist, and his fingers were gently stroking my back. Yes, rather nice. His voice was not so bad, either—at least, he sounded quite pleasant when he sighed dreamily.

He did not sound so pleasant when I bumped his stitches. It may have been an accident... then again, it may not have.

"Have a care, Miss Bennet!" he hissed, reeling backward and cupping a hand over his sore head. "I begin to think you truly are bound to torment me."

"You did not seem to mind half a moment ago."

His eyebrow quirked and his lips twitched. "My father taught me I ought always to oblige a lady."

"And did your father ever say anything about minding your own business or not trespassing on other people's land?"

"He never had to."

I set a hand on my hip. "Rather, I expect he trained you up in his own profession. Am I correct in that assumption?"

His mouth curved a little more. "More so than you can possibly imagine. But see here, Miss Bennet, I mean no harm."

"Hah! Why this interest in my father's possessions if you do not mean to steal them? Tell me you will not be sneaking through the windows at night, no doubt harassing and frightening all my sisters and even my mother in the process."

"That I can assure you with certainty. The only lady of the house I mean to 'harass' is the one standing before me, and I believe all the harassment is on your side. What do you mean by assaulting my person so, when I only asked a simple question?"

"I should have thought you would be content with what you received. That is, after all, part of your design in housebreaking, is it not? The thrill of feminine conquest?"

"Conquest, you say! I would argue that I am more a victim than anything else."

"Do you! You are terribly amusing, sir, but I must be going. My father will be most put out if I neglect to call for help, so do you prefer that I set up the cry now, or would you rather proceed down the road first?"

"But I have not asked my question."

"You did ask. I declined to answer." I turned to walk away, but he skipped round in front of me, bringing me to a halt.

"Come, Miss Bennet, it is a simple question. Despite the day's experience, I believe you to be a woman of honesty and good character, so I prefer to address you rather than alarm anyone else. I am seeking a statue—a particular type of statue—and I have reason to believe it may be in your father's possession. It ought to be twelve to eighteen inches high, and I understand it is an image of one of the gods. How long has he owned it, and how did he come by it?"

I stared, scarcely breathing. He was not asking about the vases?

But of course, he was not. That was silly! He only knew about the four at Netherfield. He could not know where they had come from, or that there were a dozen more like it in Longbourn's hidden cottage. What possible reason could he have to suspect my father? I nearly laughed at myself.

Then, I remembered *the* statue. The scandalous one, with winged Eros embracing a swooning Psyche—it made me sweat just to look up on it. Papa always claimed it was worth a dizzying sum, but I had presumed that was only more of his talk. Suppose it was true? It must be! And this rotter planned to steal it!

I cleared my throat. "We have no statues. None at all." I pivoted on my heel and went around him.

He followed me. Of course he would, the cad. "For a woman with 'no statues, none at all,' you look very pale, Miss Bennet. Are you quite certain?"

"Absolutely. Good day, Mr...." I stopped and whirled to face him. "What was your name again?"

His smile widened. "I already gave you the only name I could, for now."

I shrugged. "And it was lamentably forgettable."

He took a bold step closer. "Shall I help jog your memory? It starts with a 'W' sound."

Confused, I copied him, then gave him a cynical look. "Am I a child that you are now spelling out words for me?"

"No. I just wanted to see the shape of your mouth when you made that sound. It was well worth it."

I waved my hand in the air. "You really are incorrigible. If you truly are looking for expensive things to add to your pockets, I suggest you try Lucas Lodge."

"They have some fine possessions, do they?"

"No. Sir William has a double-barreled flintlock, and he never misses an opportunity to show it off. Would you like to see it up close?"

He narrowed his eyes and set his fists at his waist. "You really mean to play coy with me, do you not?"

I smiled.

"Very well. I suppose I shall have to seek some other means of learning what I must know." He lifted his hat. "Until we meet again, Miss Elizabeth."

Darcy

T HAT HAD BEEN A grave miscalculation.

My only intention was to gather information and learn a bit about Bennet and his ways without imposing myself in his drawing room. One did not simply arrive on the doorstep and ask to see a man's art collection. I needed some kind of approach.

I ought simply to have brought my card to the door and asked to call on the morrow. It would have been the civilized thing to do. Uncomfortable and possibly ineffective, but almost anything would have been better than kissing the man's daughter in the wood behind his house.

But one look at that brown-eyed Elizabeth Bennet, and I was no longer the master of myself.

What had I been thinking to follow her? I shouldn't wonder that I gave her a fright! Good heavens, what sort of fever had overcome me that I threw good sense, decorum, and even my dignity over, merely for the pleasure of seeing her smile? And to gather her in my arms like a lover—why, I had scarcely met the woman! Insupportable that she should already hold such power over me.

But the more astonishing revelation was my own levity in her presence. For pity's sake, I almost sounded like the rogue she took me for, and I was enjoying every second. I, Fitzwilliam Darcy of Pemberley, had always been circumspect in my associations with the fairer sex. I could not afford to flirt with abandon. In fact, I'd scarcely ever exerted myself to fix a woman's affections. Only once, to be exact—Pemberley's head cook. When I was seven years of age.

And now, just when I most wished to present myself with honor and respectability, I had another problem. Elizabeth Bennet believed I was a burglar, and nothing I said would be treated with credulity and trust.

Oh, but my foray into this little "misunderstanding" was too delicious to regret.

I pinched the bridge of my nose, trying to stave off the looming headache. It was not only the bump on the back of my head—courtesy of one Elizabeth Bennet. It was the frustration and discouragement of the predicament in which I had found myself—partly also owing to that same fiery lass.

How was I to carry out my uncle's request and work upon Mr. Bennet to preserve what ought to be a treasure for all the ages, when I could not even stop kissing the gentleman's daughter?

NINE

Elizabeth

"I HOPE WE SHALL have an excellent dinner tomorrow, Mrs. Bennet, for I have reason to expect an addition to our table."

I dragged my thoughts back from my absent reverie and looked at my father.

"We shall? It is not Mr. Bingley? Oh, my dears, we are saved! See what a good, kind father you have? Oh, I knew you were teasing me when you said—"

"It is not Mr. Bingley, but his acquaintance may prove equally gratifying. Certainly, his letters are diverting. I daresay I read them with much amusement."

"Who is it, Papa?" I asked.

He smirked at me. "It is my cousin, William Collins."

I rolled my eyes. "Oh. That one."

"What do you mean, Lizzy?"

"Eh?" Papa asked, cupping a hand to his ear.

"My dear, what is she saying?" Mama shouted. "Lizzy, you cannot mean to dismiss this poor fellow out of hand before you have ever met him. Surely!"

"What she means, Mrs. Bennet, is that she has been privy to some of my correspondence with Mr. Collins. We have had much sport in reading his missives, have we not, Lizzy?"

"He... certainly thinks well of himself," was my cautious reply.

"And well he might. It is he who shall inherit Longbourn one day."

Mama dabbed her handkerchief to her eyes. "Oh! I hate the very sound of his name. You know, girls, it is he who shall turn you out on your backsides if you do not take care to marry well ere your father dies. Come to look over his inheritance, I should think!"

"What was that? Are you going on about my imminent demise again, Mrs. Bennet? How happy for me that I am in excellent health."

"You are deaf as a post!" Mama shot back in frustration. "Next it will be your eyesight that fails, then your heart, and then who knows what shall come of us?"

"My hearing comes and goes as it pleases, and my vision is quite as sharp as it ever was. However, I thank you for reminding me of my mortality on such a regular basis. No, Collins does not come to look over his inheritance. He comes on a different sort of errand. There is much beauty to appreciate at Longbourn apart from the house, is there not?"

Mama lowered her fan. "He comes to seek a bride? Oh!" She put her hand out, waving toward Jane. "Jane, I must have you keep yourself for Mr. Bingley. You're quite the most beautiful of all your sisters, and I am sure you will fix him. But Lizzy, you would do very well for this fellow. We must make over your green morning gown, and we ought to have a look at your lace..."

"My dear, it was not my daughters I plan on displaying, although he would have to be blind not to notice them. No, no, he comes on behalf of his patroness, one Lady Catherine de Bourgh. My, the very sound of her name ought to be worth a few hundred pounds, am I right?"

"Papa," I hissed under my breath, kicking him with my toe. "I hope you are not advertising more vases for sale!"

Papa raised his glass to me and chuckled. "It seems I do not have to advertise anything. They are coming out of the woodwork now. Word of my modest little collection has spread far and wide, has it not? But not to worry, Lizzy. I know how fond you are of my vases, and it pains me to part with any of them. The butcher and the draper do like to have their accounts settled each month, and so occasionally, I permit myself to be persuaded. But you may rest easy, for Collins is not coming for one of my vases."

Jane and I shared a confused glance. "Papa, I do not understand. If he is not seeking a bride, not coming to look over the property, and not interested in one of your vases, why does he come?"

Papa's grin grew wider still. "He comes to look at my statue. It seems that Lady Catherine is a great admirer of sculpture. Moreover, she fancies herself able to compete with someone of vastly greater resources even than herself. I daresay it matters little to me, so long as her purse is as deep as she claims."

Mama clasped her hands. "My dear, it is everything splendid! Why, I never cared for that ugly thing myself, but 'tis sure to fetch thirty or forty pounds, and what couldn't I do with that?"

Papa pushed up from the table. "My imagination fails me, Mrs. Bennet."

Darcy

T HERE REALLY WAS LITTLE else for it. I would return to London and attack the problem from another angle. Because if I went to Longbourn again, unprotected, I would not give two straws for my aching head. Or my continued bachelorhood. I needed a better plan.

I departed the next morning by daybreak, and after changing horses a few times, I was in my townhouse by early afternoon. My first action was to dispatch a letter to Lord Matlock informing him I had returned. My second was to pull down the peerage books from my shelves. Something had been nibbling at my thoughts since my first research into Mr. Bennet's heritage, and I had no better idea than to chase down that figment.

I was deep in my investigation, several hours having passed, when Giles opened the door to my study. "Lord Matlock to see you, sir."

I rose from my chair. "Show him in, please."

My uncle entered, still wearing his hat and cape, such was his apparent haste to see me. "Darcy! I am glad to hear you have returned so quickly. Did you find the statue?"

"No. I suffered a rather unproductive journey to Hertfordshire. I came back to gather better intelligence. What have you?"

"A crisis, that is what I may have."

"A crisis?" I chuckled and moved to pour the earl a glass from my decanter. "Surely, it is not a matter of life and death."

"It may well be for someone. Matters have altered somewhat, and His Highness does not like to be kept out of the loop."

My hand dropped from the decanter. "His Highness? I do not understand. What could he have to do with this matter? We are not even certain there is anything to find, and the Prince Regent is already involved?"

"Bennet wrote to him and claimed to have precisely what I thought he did. He told the prince he had an ancient sculpture of Cupid and Psyche from the Parthenon. And His Highness is interested, but so is someone else."

I swirled the contents of my glass and gazed out the window. "So Bennet really does have a statue from Athens. I wondered. But who is this other party you speak of?"

"My sister! Lady Catherine is trying to cut the crown out of the Parthenon collection. Somehow, she got word of the same information as I. Richard, God bless him, alerted me she is even now trying to broker a deal with Bennet."

"A deal!" I swallowed some of my drink. "I do not like this. It is moving too fast. Can we even be certain that the piece is genuine? Something does not feel right."

"He offered it to the crown, so it must be. Unless you think it was stolen, and he means to sell it quickly?"

I looked back at my uncle, my mind still buzzing in thought. "No, nothing like that. But I was just looking at something here. Do you ever remember hearing about Robert Trenton, Viscount Elroy III?"

"No, what of him?"

I dropped a finger on the man's name in my peerage journal. "He was a close associate of Sir William Chambers and helped found the Academy of the Arts in 1768."

"Oh." Lord Matlock sounded bored. "Why mention him?"

"He is Thomas Bennet's maternal grandfather."

"Well, what of that? You think that is where Bennet obtained his collection?"

I frowned and shook my head. "Possibly. But there was something else about him... I am trying to recall. You are not familiar with his name?"

"Only vaguely. I knew Chambers in my youth, but not well."

I frowned and went back a few pages, tracing the history a bit further, but nothing triggered my memory. "I believe I will look in at the Archives. I know I recall something about Elroy."

"Some other time, Darcy. I need you back in Hertfordshire before Lady Catherine's emissary. Richard's letter said the man was nearly packed off in the dead of night, and he should arrive on the morrow, or possibly even by today."

"So soon! What do you wish me to do? Shall I try to outbid Lady Catherine?"

My uncle shook his head. "While I know you could afford it, that would not be my first choice. I was summoned to Carlton House yesterday, you must know."

I blinked. "You had a private audience with His Royal Highness?"

"I did. Apparently, he is quite set on gathering these pieces himself so that he might have the honor of donating them to the national collection once Parliament gets off their thumbs about Elgin. He has already purchased my Hercules—quite generous, he was. But if Lady Catherine gets hold of Bennet's statue, she would not sell, no matter what means the Prince employed."

"He prefers to deal with Bennet himself, then? I do not see why he would be less happy to deal with me."

"Because he had a letter from Bennet, that is why. While I do not know the contents, His Highness has got it in his royal head that the satisfaction of dealing directly with Bennet is to be unrivaled. Probably feels it would make him look magnanimous, stooping to bestow a fortune on a mere country squire or some nonsense. So, you see, Darcy, all I want you to do is act on His Highness's behalf and delay matters until the Prince himself can attend them."

I nodded slowly. "That should not be too hard. I am sure someone of Mr. Bennet's station in life would leap at the opportunity to sell his sculpture to the future king over a baronet's widow."

My uncle harrumphed in satisfaction. "You will go back tomorrow, will you not, Darcy?"

"Yes." I stroked my upper lip in thought. "Tomorrow."

But what sort of reception would I find? Well... perhaps I could find a way to speak with Mr. Bennet alone without alerting his perplexing, exhilarating daughter.

Ten

Elizabeth

WILLIAM COLLINS LOOKED AS pompous as his letters sounded. He was tall—not so tall as a certain other fellow I had just met, but what Collins lacked in sheer bulk, he made up for with awkwardness. His shoe caught on the hall rug twice, he insisted I had been introduced as Mary and that Lydia been presented to him as Jane, and he commented at least four times on how "quaint" and "not over-pretentious" the drawing room was. That was all before he had even sat down.

"I have been most fortunate in my patroness," he announced as Mrs. Hill brought the tea. "Why, I cannot imagine being treated with greater deference. Her ladyship has placed in my care all matters of import with the estate, save, of course, those which are best attended only by her noble self. Her Ladyship taught me all the particulars of her ways, down to the very minutest detail of how large of a joint my cook should purchase for the Sunday meal and the exact spacing of the shelves in my closets for the best storage. I declare, nothing is too small for her notice, so patronizing is she. And so she has taught me to be, such that she now entrusts me with the business dearest to her heart."

"Oh, how marvelous!" my mother praised him. "Do you hear that, Lizzy? He is well-thought-of. A man with responsibilities! Very respectable, sir, very fine."

I gave my mother a thin smile. "I am sure it is, Mama."

"Tell me," Papa said, "is it not passing rare that a parson ought to concern himself with matters beyond his parish? Feeding souls is one thing, but how flattering that you should also now oversee joints and shelves at her ladyship's pleasure."

Collins nodded and set his teacup on the cart. Or he tried to, but it was only by Hill pushing the cart under his hand at the last second he did not drop the thing on the floor.

"I am honored, indeed. And now, Mr. Bennet, it is my very great pleasure to act on Lady Catherine's behalf in this most vital of matters. Why, it was only last week when she summoned me to her private sitting room—I am the only outsider permitted to call on her there—and besought my counsel on the matter at hand. 'Mr. Collins,' she said, 'do you make haste to put down all you know about Mr. Bennet, his family, and his prospects. Bring them to me by the morrow, and I shall send you to him with my offer.' That was what she said, and, my dear Mr. Bennet, here I am."

My father slid his gaze to me, his expression dry. "I am flattered that this distinguished person could take such an interest in someone so inconsequential as myself. What do I know of ladyships and shelves and joints? Truly, sir, I am humbled by her condescension."

Mr. Collins bowed his head, beaming proudly. "Her ladyship does us both honor. And now, my good sir, might I be so bold as to request the pleasure of seeing this masterpiece in your possession?"

Papa suppressed a chortle as he raised his hand. "Mr. Hill, will you please bring it in?"

I thought Collins would perspire and gasp his last when our old butler pushed in a second tea cart with a draped figure perched on top. A clever bit of theatrics from Papa, as always, for never is one so inclined to beg for the pleasure of buying something as when he cannot see what it is he means to buy.

"Lady Catherine is prepared to pay seventy-five pounds for it!" he cried.

Papa arrested himself halfway out of his chair. "But my good sir, you have not even seen it yet."

Mama started fanning herself. "Seventy-five pounds! Goodness me, girls. You are saved!" she whispered.

Collins gripped the armrests of his chair and fairly lunged to his feet. "I pray you, sir, lift the veil and relieve my suspense!"

I cast Jane a worried glance. With the way this Collins fellow was lumbering about, it would be a wonder if he did not knock the sculpture over before they ever settled on a price.

Ever the showman, Papa lifted the white cloth with a flourish. "There you are, Mr. Collins. Is it not everything Lady Catherine could possibly have imagined?"

Collins tiptoed toward it, his mouth hanging open and a long lock of unkempt hair dropping over his eyes. Such had been his eagerness to marvel at the thing. Truly, it *was* worthy of admiration. I tilted my head and tried to imagine seeing it for the first time.

It was large enough to grace a mantel or a pedestal in a grand house. If I placed my fingertips on the table beside it and measured it with my forearm, the tips of Eros' wings came just above my elbow. The marble was scarred here and there, and the tip of one wing was missing, which only added to its value, according to Papa.

Eros, or Cupid, however one preferred to call him, was truly a figure to behold—*all* of him. And the way he was cradling his lover, with his hand upon... well, that much does not entirely bear repeating, but it had put many a fancy in *my* head. I can say that much with confidence. Euphoric rapture cried out in the lines of their faces and the postures of their bodies, and the figures were rendered in exquisite detail. Clearly, the work of a master.

Papa said there was no way to know who had originally crafted the marble statue, as it was so very old. He claimed to have obtained it only in the last year from some unknown collector, but I had always nursed some foggy memory of finding something similar in his hidden cottage when I was very young. But that must be mere imagination, for what purpose would Papa have in not telling me where it had come from?

I still wondered what he was about, purchasing something that certainly must have been quite dear when Longbourn did not have deep coffers. Mama was always complaining that she needed more pin money, and our gowns had all been made over more times than they ought to have been. But if this Lady Catherine was willing to pay a handsome price, perhaps I could forgive my father for making such a lavish expenditure.

"One hundred pounds," Collins whispered reverently.

Papa arched a brow. "Well, now, Collins, I had not quite settled on whether I ought to sell it."

"Oh!" my mother scoffed. "Mr. Bennet, how you trifle with me. Of course, you will sell it! He has offered one hundred pounds! Are you mad?"

"I must be, my dear. No, no, I quite enjoy having this on my desk as I write my little letters of business and so on. I'm afraid you will have to tell Lady Catherine that I will consider her offer."

I snickered, and Jane nudged me with the toe of her house slipper. Papa loved bartering almost as much as he loved his pottery.

Collins' face changed hues, and his mouth gaped helplessly. "But Her Ladyship said I ought not to return until I had made all the arrangements! She will be most seriously displeased if I do not satisfy her."

"Well! Then if you must, you are welcome to remain as our guest some days. Hill will make you comfortable. Oh, Jane, Lizzy? Were you still planning to go walking this afternoon? I wonder, as Collins here is to stay with us, perhaps you could show him around Meryton. I am sure you would enjoy that, would you not, Mr. Collins?"

Collins had his back to me, but his disappointment at not receiving immediate gratification played through every clumsy bone in his body. "Yes. Yes, that will do, Mr. Bennet. I thank you for your gracious offer. But I cannot stay more than... a week. Yes, a week. Lady Catherine is expecting me."

"And we cannot disappoint Lady Catherine, can we? We will talk again on the morrow, Mr. Collins. Meanwhile, girls run along and get your pelisses and your bonnets and your muffs. Good lasses. Enjoy your outing!"

I pierced my father with a dangerous look, but he only grinned back at me as he removed his spectacles. How very tidy he had fixed everything! Collins would now be even more desperate to make a deal with each hour that passed, but the burden of entertaining him had fallen on Jane and me. One could be certain that our younger sisters would be of no help.

"I'm going to scream, Jane," I whispered.

"Not here. You'll scare Collins, and he'll knock the statue over," she murmured back.

I sighed. "Well, come on. We may as well get this over with. With any luck, we can outpace him to town, so we shan't have to listen to his praises of Lady Catherine."

Darcy

I HAD NOT MUCH time. The Royal Archive did not open their vault to just anyone, and I had no "Lord" in front of my name. It was to my everlasting relief that the keeper of the records treasury turned out to be Viscount Rogan, an old friend from Cambridge who had relied heavily on me to pass his mathematics classes.

"One hour, Darcy," he cautioned me. "And I cannot permit you to remove anything."

"I would not dream of it. If you will direct me to the volumes I speak of, I will be on my way as swiftly as I have come."

I couldn't even say what I had been looking for. It was just a vague memory, something I had overheard from my father, I believed. But Viscount Elroy III had some scandal attached to him. I was sure of it. Unfortunately, that is not the sort of thing one finds written in a book of official records. If I could just find something to trigger the rest of my memory...

But an hour came and went, and all I had to show for my effort was that I now knew how many paintings by Michelangelo the man had brought from Italy. In fact, Elroy seemed to have been obsessed with Michelangelo. When Rogan came to run me out, I was ready to confess that it had been a wild goose chase. What did I really expect to find?

"Did you discover what you sought?" Rogan asked.

"No. But I suppose it might be worth asking if you know what came of Elroy's collection after his death. I understand he had no son, and the estate and title passed to the crown."

"That's all I know."

I sighed. "A pity. From what I can gather, he had little to pass to his daughter, and she was forced to settle on a modest country squire. What came of his fortune? I would expect all his Michelangelos went with the estate. I should like to have seen them one day."

"Ah, yes. You know, I believe His Majesty has a few paintings in his collection, but I have not been privileged to admire them. Oh! That does bring something to mind. There is that small Cupid sculpture here by Michelangelo. Something of a scandal it once was, but that only adds to the value now."

"How so?"

"Well, he faked it."

I stopped as if stung by something. "Come again?"

Rogan laughed. "Michelangelo faked it. He carved it so it looked just like something the old masters would have done, and then he buried it for a while to age it. Then he sold it to some high-ranking Italian Cardinal!"

"What? I never heard this."

"Oh, yes. Quite the stir he caused. The broker was ruined in the deal, but Michelangelo himself became recognized for his ability to copy the Classic sculptors. It made his career, no questions about it. No one cared that he had committed fraud because they loved his talent. I suppose one never knows, eh?"

I narrowed my eyes and continued walking. "No, I suppose not."

And then I jerked to a halt.

"Something the matter, Darcy?"

I sucked in a breath. "No. I just remembered why I knew Elroy's name." I offered my hand. "Thank you for your help, Rogan."

He frowned and shrugged. "Anytime, Darcy."

T HE NEXT DAY, I took a carriage that did not bear the Darcy crest when I returned to Meryton. I could not say why I felt such reserve. Certainly, I would need to appear credible to Mr. Bennet when I arrived, but I would have little trouble proving myself. And I wanted to prove myself—to his daughter, at least. Someday. A proper introduction, with my real name, so that I might consider knowing her better, and so she might consider not wounding me when I spoke to her.

But not yet. It was the misunderstandings cultivated by my previous visit to the area, I suppose. Better to protect my name for now, in case it was necessary to redirect any more confusion.

Tempting as it was to think of dallying with that Bennet daughter, I would need to avoid her at all costs today. Not only could her first impressions of me thwart my present mission, but... well, hang it all. If I spent another unchaperoned minute in her company, I would soon find myself with a wife.

So it was that I stepped down from my carriage at the Meryton inn, satisfied with my plan and confident in its success. I would take a luncheon and refresh myself. Then I would ride out to Longbourn in style and ask to call on Mr. Bennet.

It would be afternoon, the time when many young ladies went calling or took their constitutionals. I should be able to find the man in his study and have a private conversation before any feminine influences hindered me. I caught up my walking stick, set my hat on my head, and walked to the inn's door.

"I do not believe it."

Heat crawled over my shoulders and up the back of my neck at the sound of that familiar voice. *Oh, no.* I turned slowly.

Elizabeth Bennet was standing on the walk, a new-looking book tucked to her chest and her chocolate curls drifting gently across her lips in the afternoon breeze. I gulped. It was bloody unfair.

As quickly as I had nearly lost my composure, I jerked to regain it. I doffed my hat and bowed. "Good afternoon, Miss Bennet."

She shook her head in disbelief. "I thought you left town. I had pleasant dreams last night and everything, thinking the windows and locks on my house were safe from your meddling."

"And so they are. I am a man of my word, Miss Bennet."

She burst into a laugh, her eyes sparking merrily. I had not known her eyes could catch the sun quite like that. I knotted my fist on my walking stick, but my fingers trembled to recall how soft her skin had felt.

"And why, sir, should I believe you? Hmm? You are dressed very finely today, I see. You must have had a productive journey. What did you sell this time? Mrs. Marcus's silver spoons?"

"Spoons? Why would I even bother? No, what I am after is something far more majestic. One could even say... tempting."

Her eyes never changed, but one brow arched. "You seem to be a man of many temptations."

"Just one, Miss Bennet."

"Then you are still trying to learn about my father's statue?"

"Your father does have something of interest to me."

She turned nonchalantly to her book; her gloved fingers brushing over the cover. "I suppose it might interest you to learn that he has already sold it. You are too late."

Dash it all. I tried not to let the disappointment flicker across my face. "I would find that mildly interesting, yes. I was hoping to be the first to it. May I ask who purchased it?"

She tipped her chin up to me and smiled, serene in her victory. "Do you see that great, tall gentleman over there? His name is Mr. Collins, and he is terribly ferocious. And strong, too—why, they say he is a veritable ox." She pointed to a fellow across the street who was walking with two young ladies, carrying their parcels.

I turned to watch him. The man's gaze was fixed on the "Meryton Drapers" sign on the building, and he failed to pick up his feet when the young ladies tried to drag him inside. Consequently, he met with a rather hard fall, knocking off his hat and probably bruising his chin.

"Oh, Mr. Collins! You have crushed my new bonnet!" cried one girl.

He picked himself up, apologizing profusely and trying to conceal the fact that he had ripped a great hole in the knee of his trousers.

I turned back to Elizabeth. "Yes, I see. He is a savage, to be sure. I daren't face him if I value my life."

She cleared her throat. "Yes, well, he only negotiates on behalf of a very important person named Lady Catherine de Bourgh. I understand she is quite wealthy and powerful. I would not wish to offend her if I were you."

"No." I shook my head. "Nor would I, if I were you, for I am well acquainted with this Lady Catherine. One might even say we share a connection of some long standing. I tell you what—I cannot be the reason for Lady Catherine's displeasure. Mr. Collins and the statue are quite safe from me."

She drew a breath, her chest lifting and her shoulders relaxing. "May I have your word on that, sir?"

"Of course. So far as it depends on me, the statue will be delivered to Lady Catherine's keeping, unmolested. That ought to make Carruthers happy."

A fine line appeared between her eyes. "Carruthers?"

"Oh, did you not hear his name before? Ah, no matter. Standard, really."

Those fine eyes narrowed, and she shook her head. "I cannot imagine why I would trust you for a second, but let us imagine I do. Who is this Carruthers person?"

"I am surprised Mr. Collins did not mention it. He is one of the foremost experts on ancient art in all London. Lady Catherine's greatest pleasure is in hearing the praise of others."

Elizabeth snorted and rolled her eyes. "Which explains why she chose my cousin as her parson."

"Indeed! To her, there is nothing so fine that the pleasure of owning it is not enhanced by paying others to admire it. Or to appraise it."

She blinked, and her lips parted. "What is this?"

"It is the way she has always conducted her transactions. Nothing unusual, to be sure. And if she likes what she hears, why, she will sing your father's praises to the skies for years. But if she does not—well, I recall one poor chap who tried to sell her a retouched painting." I shook my head. "I still think of his family from time to time."

Elizabeth's book slipped from her hand. I bent to pick it up for her, but she hurried to gather it in the same instant. Her bonnet flicked off my hat, and her head collided with mine—right on the wound from the day before.

Stars exploded in my brain. I had not known just how tender it still was, but I came close to collapsing from the pain. As it was, I nearly lost command of my faculties there on the walk before the inn. "Egad, Miss Elizabeth," I gasped. "Will you ever stop damaging me?"

She was scrambling to pick up my hat and pick up her book and look across the street all at once. "I beg your pardon, sir, truly. Jane!" She waved at someone just coming out of the draper's shop. "Lydia, Kitty! We must return home at once!"

"Why the rush? I thought we were finally having a pleasant conversation."

"Another time, sir. I really must fly." She brandished my hat, gave it a glance over to determine which was the front, and then smashed it onto my head herself. I couldn't help it—I moaned like a baby when she clapped it down, hard, on my stitched scalp.

"Goodbye, sir! I hope we do not meet again, but if we do... don't... don't steal anything." She waved her book at me and ran, the strings of her bonnet trailing behind her.

I was still panting in pain, and I had to lean against the door of the inn to catch myself. I might have just won the time I needed to speak with Mr. Bennet, but why did I feel like I had actually lost that exchange? The woman was... terrifying.

Eleven

Elizabeth

Papa was not in his study when we returned to Longbourn. That was no surprise. I knew precisely where to find him, but ridding myself of Mr. Collins proved difficult. Lydia and Kitty had gone to call on their friend Maria Lucas—probably so they did not have to walk back with the rest of us. Mary slipped into the parlor to bang away on some concerto, and Mama called Jane to her sitting room "to ease her poor nerves."

Thus, I was forced to take tea with the oaf, my eyes on the clock every second as he recounted the many splendors of Rosings Park, the seat of Lady Catherine de Bourgh. However, I am not formed to suffer in silence. If I could do nothing but play the hostess for a quarter of an hour, I would make the best of it by learning what I wished to know.

"Lady Catherine sounds like a woman of exquisite taste," I murmured as I sipped from my cup. *There.* I had but to observe that much, and he would rattle on for some minutes, unaided, while I enjoyed my tea.

I was not disappointed. I learned all about the glazing on her windows and the costliness of her fireplace, and the lavish quality of her Turkish rugs, not to mention a dozen more trivialities I cared nothing for. I had time to finish my cup before I could put another word in.

"And has she much art to grace her home?" I asked. "Many portraits by the masters, no doubt, but what of sculpture?"

"Oh!" Collins set down his cup and acted as if his heart had grown faint. "My fair cousin, you can have no notion of the variety and magnificence of her collection! Why, I once counted the pieces in her gallery, and they numbered over *thirty!*"

"Indeed! I suppose a lady of such a grand estate with so many wondrous treasures has little need for more."

"But you are mistaken, cousin! Lady Catherine is a curator of fine art. She accepts it as her sacred duty to preserve and guard the great masterpieces of the ages from those who would not appreciate and protect them."

"Truly, she is a grand lady," I whispered, my eyes wide.

"I flatter myself when I say you can have no possible concept of her beneficence. Only this year, she secured a sculpture to rival the very one in Mr. Bennet's keeping, and she desires nothing more than to set them together, as book-ends in her library. *There,* what do you think of *that*, my fair cousin?"

"She has a library, does she? What sorts of books does she keep?"

"Only what is suitable to a lady of her station, of course! Everything is bound in fine leather and gold leaf and tastefully shelved to best highlight and augment their quality."

"Ah. A true book lover, then," I sighed. I never could abide a library that was kept as a showpiece rather than a well-organized repository of wisdom and delight.

"Naturally! But the true splendor of her library is not the books themselves, of course, but the mere aspect of the room. I cannot possibly do justice to the beauty, the graciousness—"

"That is all well and good," I interrupted, tiring of his prattle. "But what honor is there in a house, be it the library or the gallery, if only one person exists to appreciate it?"

Collins put his hand to his chest again. "Oh, but that is not true! She has a daughter, the heiress of Rosings, and a fine creature she is! Alas, her health is not robust, but if it were, I can think of nothing that would prevent her from becoming the fairest star of the *ton*. Indeed—"

"Oh, I was not talking about family. They are obliged to compliment one's little hobby regardless of their actual opinions. But does Lady Catherine not display her collection to others who might admire it?" I poured a second cup of tea for him.

"Ah! Forgive me. I misunderstood. Naturally, Lady Catherine appreciates a kindred mind of discerning taste. To that end, when she acquires a new treasure, she always summons one of unparalleled expertise and acumen to affirm its quality and to bask in its splendor."

My hand quaked on the teapot. "She does? Who is this person?"

Collins sipped from his cup and then whispered, as if in reverence. "His name is Carruthers, and his opinion weighs greatly with her ladyship. Why, I have it on good authority that his expertise is valued far and wide for the exactness and accuracy of his judgment."

I blinked. *Carruthers!* That William person had been telling the truth! And now Papa might have got us in an awful fix. Oh, I *knew* something like this would happen someday!

I set my cup aside, trying to steady my breathing. "If you will forgive me, Mr. Collins, I'm suddenly feeling slightly indisposed. I think I must lie down for a while."

"But of course! Far be it from me to disregard the delicacy of a lady's constitution. Why, as I have always assured Lady Catherine when her dearest daughter Anne—"

I heard no more. I doubt Mr. Collins even realized that when I left him, I did not go upstairs to my room for a lie-down. I pulled on my bonnet and my walking boots and ran outside.

"PAPA, THIS IS VERY serious! I wish you would listen to me."

"Indeed, my child, I have done little else." Papa wedged the glass into his eye and picked up his paintbrush. "What do you think of this one, my dear? Just a little touch... here... And there. I believe I will put it in the drawing room this evening and then inform Mr. Collins that it is not for sale at any price. I warrant he will offer a tidy sum of lady Catherine's money for this to go along with the sculpture, do you not think?"

"Papa, that is just the trouble! Whatever Lady Catherine purchases will be inspected by one of London's foremost experts! Can you tell me for certain that the statue is genuine? We cannot risk—"

"But of course it is genuine!" Papa snorted, his paintbrush dripping in his hand. "You can see it, touch it, can you not?"

I pressed my fingers to my temples. "But where did it come from? Did you really buy it last year in Scotland from some famous Greek collector?"

Papa lowered his brush and sighed. "If you are so insistent on knowing, the answer is no. I did not buy it from Lord Elgin. He had a few smaller sculptures like this, but most of his were bits and pieces of life-sized statues and friezes from the Parthenon and similar structures."

"So, where did yours come from?"

He dipped his brush in the paint and squinted at his vase again. "It belonged to my mother, bequeathed to her by her father. Heaven only knows where he got it. But what does that matter?"

I gasped. "So, why would you say you got it from Lord Elgin?"

"Oh! As to that, why not? He had a few things *like* mine, as I said. Parliament may not even know about them, but if they did, I am sure they would want them. So, why not dangle the bait a bit? Hah, what do you think? I called it a statue of Cupid rather than Eros. Same god, two different names, and who am I to say which the sculptor wanted?"

I leaned both hands on my father's work table and stared him in the eyes. "Does Lady Catherine believe you are selling her a Greek statue from this Lord Elgin's collection?"

"Of course she does. It is twice as valuable with his name attached to it because everyone knows he brought back a hoard from Greece. Why, the scandal of it—whether he bought it legally—is just as alluring as the collection itself. How do you think I should demand such a price for it otherwise?"

"That is exactly my point! Lady Catherine will discover the truth and know you have defrauded her. She is powerful, Papa. And at one whiff of suspicion from her, everyone who has ever purchased one of your vases will also demand some redress. Do you not see how our family could be ruined? Think of poor Uncle Gardiner, who brokered the transactions in good faith!"

"Oh, Lizzy, you place far too much confidence in these 'experts.' What do they know?"

I crossed my arms. "And you have far too little. There must be some way of discovering whether your *Eros and Psyche* is a genuine antique or a worthless replica."

"Worthless! Something so beautiful as that? And it is Cupid, in case anyone asks."

"No one cares about beauty, Papa. They want something prestigious to brag about. Is there a way to be sure of yours?"

He sighed and tossed his brush into a pot. "Oh, perhaps, if a man knew his marble well enough. There are always things to be found, but one expert says one thing, another says something different, so who knows?"

"Does your statue appear genuine beyond a reasonable suspicion?"

He picked up a rag to wipe down his hands. "If no one thinks to look closely at the color in the marble veins. But I cannot think why they would."

I sagged onto the little stool at his work table. "Oh, Papa. You must tell Lady Catherine you have decided against selling. Surely, the risk—"

Papa chuckled and patted me on the shoulder. "But your mother already has the money spent. How do you think I mean to pad your dowry? Not to worry, my child. Lady Catherine is not the only interested party, to be sure."

"Would anyone else handle the matter differently?"

He only smiled and held the door for me. "Come, Lizzy. Let us go up for tea before someone thinks to look for us."

I stopped outside, my head spinning. I desperately needed a normal conversation with someone rational, and I'd made poor Jane nervous enough already. "Actually, I believe I will walk over to Lucas Lodge. I would like to speak to Charlotte about something."

"Ah, well. I suppose the rest of us will have to entertain Mr. Collins until dinner, eh?" He winked. "Enjoy yourself, my child."

I kissed my father on the cheek, then turned up a different path. I walked to Lucas Lodge on leaden feet, my stomach churning with worry. Papa was playing a terrible game of chance, gambling on not being discovered. One day, his luck would run out, and it would be too late for all of us.

Darcy

I STEPPED DOWN FROM my carriage at Longbourn and cast an eye over the house. It had never impressed me as a stately home, but it seemed a little less opulent on a closer appraisal. I doubted not that Lord Matlock's offer would be met with interest. With five daughters to marry off and a house in a slight state of disrepair, surely Mr. Bennet would welcome the money.

But that was only if all matters were favorable.

I walked toward the door, but before I could reach it, the gentleman himself appeared from around the corner of the house. He looked to have been out for a leisurely stroll, wearing a greatcoat that had fallen out of fashion at least ten years earlier and a hat more suited to inspecting the fields than going out in public. Perhaps that was precisely what he had been doing, because there were traces of mud on his boots, as well.

He lifted his hat at my approach and smiled. "Good afternoon, sir. You look as if you have just set down off a carriage from London. I hope you have not lost your way."

I touched my hat and offered a crisp bow. "Not if I presently stand before Mr. Bennet of Longbourn. I beg your pardon for arriving without notice. Fitzwilliam Darcy, at your service, sir."

He nodded, his gaze sweeping me from top hat to boot tips. "Thomas Bennet at yours. How may I help you, sir?"

"I only ask a word for now, perhaps more, if you are agreeable."

Bennet's smile widened. "I am happy to oblige, but first, a question. Are you a bachelor?"

I blinked and drew back. "I beg your pardon?"

"It is a simple enough question. Have you a wife, or are you in the market for one?"

"Why, I... neither, sir. I say, this is a rather impertinent question."

He chuckled. "Nay, for you do not know Mrs. Bennet. If you have not a wife already, she would be certain that you left with one. Perhaps you would prefer if I did not invite you inside but instead offered to walk with you up the lane. Will that suit?"

I glanced at the door of the house. My greatest fear on this errand had been to encounter Elizabeth Bennet, and this option might save me from that fate. "By all means, sir."

I fell into step beside him, and he guided me toward a little wild pleasure garden to the south of the house. "Now, then. What was your business, Mr. Darcy?"

I clasped my hands behind my back. "I come at the behest of Lord Matlock, who, as you may know, is a Member of Parliament."

"Ah! He sounds an important fellow."

"Indeed, for he has the confidence of the Prince of Wales himself."

Mr. Bennet gave a low whistle. "Then I wonder how a humble farmer like myself could be of interest to such a man."

I glanced at him. "You must know. The prince received a letter that you have in your private possession a small statue that was brought from Athens with Elgin's marbles. His Highness is interested if the statue is everything you claim."

The man clucked and frowned. "Indeed, I have such a sculpture. I would be happy to show it to you, but you must know I have already received a prior offer. I should not like to default on my word, sir."

"Then you have accepted the offer?"

Mr. Bennet smiled, his eyes twinkling, and suddenly, my mind was filled with the eyes of another Bennet. "I did not say I had accepted, but I have not refused."

I stopped walking and pulled out a leather purse from my coat. "I have a note here from Lord Matlock, which may induce you to consider his offer more carefully than the one you already have."

He grunted and took the note with a smile. Then his smile faded, and his cheek twitched. He read it over for at least a full minute, then folded the note and drew a careful breath. "You make your point most eloquently, Mr. Darcy. I believe I must consider it. But are you certain you do not wish to see it first? You may be purchasing a lump of clay for His Royal Highness."

I tucked the note back into my coat. "Naturally, I would see it myself before I could assure you of the offer."

"Yes, yes, you would. Well, come, Mr. Darcy. I believe I can keep Mrs. Bennet from breathing down your neck if I tell her your purpose in coming was to feather her nest a bit. May I offer you something? Come all the way from London. I shouldn't wonder if you were thirsty."

I hesitated. Mr. Bennet seemed agreeable enough, but the last thing I needed at this present juncture was another encounter with his daughter. No matter how my body tingled at the idea. "Are you certain you are quite at your leisure? I would not wish to interrupt any... family... events."

He chuckled. "And what sort of 'family events' could I be expecting? No, you are quite safe from my wife. My daughters, however! You should be safe enough from Jane and Mary, but I daresay if you encounter Lydia, your wisest course is to run back to your carriage as swiftly as your legs may carry you. And Lizzy! It would be better if she did not know your business or even that walking stick would not be sufficient protection."

"I can quite imagine."

"Indeed. Oh! There she comes now."

My heart plunged into my boots, and I looked urgently up the lane. Indeed, two women were walking our way, but too far distant for the unaided eye to recognize their faces. Except that I already knew that pale lavender gown and that animated way of walking. It was, assuredly, the very person I dreaded most.

"Oh, dear," Mr. Bennet lamented. "I thought her away from the house all afternoon. She must have encountered Miss Lucas on the way and invited her back here. I am afraid, Mr. Darcy, that I cannot vouch for your safety." And then he laughed as if it were funny.

It wasn't.

I swallowed. Stared at that light, airy figure bouncing down the lane, with her bonnet shading her eyes and her bubbling laugh carrying to my ears like music. And I panicked. "Do you know, Mr. Bennet, I believe I will belay that request to see your sculpture."

"Are you certain? You do not wish to disappoint Lord Matlock or His Royal Highness, I presume."

I shook my head, my mouth running dry. "No. Your personal guarantee will be quite sufficient. I will send word to Lord Matlock that you will entertain his offer."

"Well! That was simple enough. I daresay Lady Catherine and William Collins will be very much put out, but if you can assure me I shall not be releasing the bird in my hand only to beat an empty bush, then I am quite content."

"You will not be disappointed, sir. Forgive me, but I believe I will take my leave. You may look for further word from Lord Matlock in a day or two."

He bowed from the waist. "It is a pleasure doing business with you, Mr. Darcy."

I returned the gesture. "You as well, Mr. Bennet."

I could not walk back to the carriage quickly enough. It was fortunate that I had changed my coat and hat before coming, else Elizabeth could have recognized my clothing from afar. I hoped she did not already know my gait and bearing as intimately as I apparently knew hers. The ladies passed a hedge just before I reached my carriage, and by the time they had emerged, I was safely away.

And all that remained was to castigate myself for promising a purse that would impoverish an entire English county for a sculpture I had not even seen in person.

TWELVE

Elizabeth

"WHO WAS THAT, PAPA?"

I took off my wrap at the door and poked my head around the door to my father's library. He was just settling into his chair and pulling out a sheaf of writing paper. He looked up with a dazed expression.

"Who was what, my pet?"

I pointed toward the window. "The gentleman who was just here with the fine carriage. What did he want?"

A weak, euphoric smile warmed his face. "That, my dear, was a miracle. Now, run along and entertain Miss Lucas. I have a letter to write. Oh! If you see Mr. Collins wandering about, tell him I am busy, please."

I narrowed my eyes, but stepped from the doorway. "Very well." Whatever had he got up to now? Frowning, I went to the drawing room where Charlotte was settling herself by the hearth.

"Was it something important?" she asked when I sat beside her.

I shook my head. "Who knows? He has been behaving even more oddly than usual."

"Speaking of odd! Have you heard of what happened to Mrs. Purvis? I overheard her talking to my mother this morning. She said that she went outside to find a strange man just coming out of her hen house!"

I stiffened. "What sort of strange man?"

"Well, according to her, he was a beastly, tall man with dark hair and a terrible leer."

I nibbled my bottom lip. Mrs. Purvis tended to exaggerate. Why, only a fortnight ago, she claimed an entire herd of her neighbor's cows had got loose and trampled her herb garden, but when the matter was investigated, it was found to be only two small calves nibbling on the parsley. But this report of a stranger in the hen house sounded too familiar for me to dismiss it.

"What happened? Did she speak to him?"

"Oh, as to that," Charlotte laughed, "she said his accent sounded northern, but beyond that, she refused to give Mama a full account. I only heard a few whispers, and I saw her nodding most emphatically. If I had to guess, I would say our romantic rascal is still up to his old tricks, eh?"

My mouth tasted like sawdust. That bounder! That creeping cad! How dare he kiss and flirt with me and then move shamelessly on to the next conquest? Why, he was no better than the duplicitous jaybird, flitting from one tree to another and all the time disguising his true nature. Oh, if I ever saw him again, he would wish I *had* brained him when I had the chance!

"Did he steal anything from Mrs. Purvis?" I heard myself ask.

"Why, of course! We never hear of this thief but that he stole something. She said he took Mr. Purvis's best greatcoat and a clutch of coins that were hidden under a jar in the hen house."

I squinted at the floor. He had never actually stolen anything when I was around him. Yes, those sounded like things a regular thief might steal, but I couldn't quite picture William taking Mr. Purvis's greatcoat. He already dressed far more richly than Mr. Purvis ever had. And he hadn't struck me as the kind to loot for coins. Every time I had spoken with him, it had been about some sort of art. He was the most peculiar burglar I ever heard of.

"Did he not take any paintings or perhaps the China? I know they have that very fine Gainsborough hanging in the parlor, and that beautiful Wedgwood Queens Ware she always keeps on display and never uses. Why would he not have made an attempt for those?"

"Oh, you are very silly, Lizzy. Steal a bulky painting or a fragile teapot from the house when he could have ready money just by raiding the chicken coop? You have a strange concept of what a burglar's job is."

"Yes, I suppose so. You are right—if a man had no scruples about stealing, it would make more sense simply to take the coins."

"Privately?" Charlotte grinned and looked over her shoulder, then bent her head close to mine. "I hope I catch him trying to break into Lucas Lodge."

I slanted an eyebrow at her. "Why would that be?"

"I hear he's handsome, and so far, every lady he has stolen from can only blush when she is asked about their encounter. I am *fearfully* curious how he manages it!"

"I have a fair idea," I retorted dryly.

Charlotte giggled. "So do I, but that does not mean I do not wish to test my theory."

"You are a dreadful hoyden!"

"No. I am only practical. I am twenty-seven years old, and no man has ever kissed me."

"Oh, come now. You cannot mean *never*. Why, every six-teen-year-old plays kissing games at house parties and contrives a way to 'accidentally' get caught under the mistletoe."

"Yes, and I was always chosen as the lookout in case Mama should walk in." She sighed. "No one ever wanted to stand under the mistle-toe with me because my eyes are pale, and I had too many freckles. Likely none ever shall, but if I should encounter this amorous bandit, I expect he would do the job creditably. And now, you have not yet told me about—"

Charlotte broke off when we heard Hill open the door to some-one in the hall. Heavy, uneven footsteps followed, then Mr. Collins' ponderous shape filled the doorway to the sitting room. He was out of breath from too much walking, and he dabbed his forehead with a limp handkerchief. "Ah, cousin Elizabeth! Is your father at his leisure? I should very much like to speak with him."

"I believe he was tending to some correspondence and wished for privacy."

He looked crestfallen. "It is most urgent that I speak with him. Lady Catherine will not countenance much delay in coming to the point. I—"

"Mr. Collins," I interrupted, "allow me to introduce you to my good friend, Charlotte Lucas. Charlotte, this is my father's cousin, William Collins."

He barely looked at Charlotte, but she, most decidedly, was looking at him. I could not say why, for he was not much to look at. But Charlotte was smiling most indecorously and even touching the curls at the side of her face as she greeted him.

"I am *most* pleased to make your acquaintance, sir," she crooned. "My, what a splendid speaking voice you have. Your parishioners are fortunate, indeed, to have the pleasure of hearing you each Sunday."

He nodded absently. "Yes, they are. Lady Catherine said as much. Miss Elizabeth, have you any notion of how long Mr. Bennet will be? I cannot delay long."

"Oh, but would you not be more comfortable waiting here with us?" Charlotte offered. "The pot is still hot, and I would be happy to serve you myself. You look like a man who takes two or perhaps three lumps with his tea."

"Three," he agreed as he pulled his pocket watch out. He never even looked up when Charlotte ran her tongue lightly over her upper lip at him.

I blinked at her. "*Charlotte!*" I hissed. "Whatever are you *doing?*"

"Quiet, Lizzy," she whispered back, her mouth scarcely breaking from that ridiculous leer. "I would settle for a parson if I cannot have the burglar."

"Oh, for pity's sake. He's barely human. He slurps his tea!"

"But I bet he can kiss. Look at those plump preacher's lips! And from the looks of things..." she titled her head to examine him from all angles. "He could use some instruction in the art. I think I might actually be more experienced than he is."

"You just told me you had never kissed anyone!"

"Exactly." She kept smiling and touching her hair, but Collins hardly noticed. He was too busy checking his pocket watch and staring across the hall at the door to my father's library. After a few minutes, he appeared to give up and shuffled up the stairs.

"Charlotte, you cannot be serious," I chided her.

"Who says I have to be serious? Admit it, Lizzy. If a handsome and charming man should walk up to you and take you in his arms, you cannot tell me you would not kiss him back."

I swallowed and felt the blood draining from my face. "Of-of c-course not."

"Hah! You are lying, Lizzy. I can always tell when your eyes get big like that, and your ears turn red. What is his name?"

"Name? Whatever are you talking ab—"

"I'm talking about you not being so saintly as you would have the rest of us think. I saw how your eyes lit up, and your teeth started grinding when I brought up that burglar! Tell me the truth. Have you had an encounter with him?"

"No!" I scoffed. That was true. I'd had a *few*... 'encounters' with him. "And anyway, why would I hide something like that? The scoundrel! He ought to be hung by his fancy boots and flogged until his curly hair turns straight. I've no sympathy for him."

"Oh, yes," Charlotte agreed. "I can see that."

"And another thing! Why would I like a man who would go around kissing someone like Mildred Purvis? She has to be forty years of age!"

"I hear men appreciate a woman who knows how to kiss back." Charlotte shrugged and donned a wicked grin. "But that's only hearsay. By the by, I never heard that this burglar had curly hair. Now that *is* a useful bit of information, is it not? Are his curls tight and frizzy, or the loose, luxurious sort? Were they cropped short or long and tousled?"

I narrowed my eyes. "I think I hear your mother calling."

Charlotte laughed and gathered her skirts to stand. "Very well. I expect a full report, just in case anyone tries to break into Longbourn. Be sure to guard the silver, Lizzy."

I shook my head as she collected her hat and went out. The little Jezebel! I'd never any notion that Charlotte Lucas could be... well, so much like Lydia. If she only knew what this thief who so fascinated her was really like! Why, he was...

He was...

I leaned against the side of the sofa, knotted my fingers around my knee, and gazed at the ceiling. He *was* pretty scrumptious. In a wicked, terrible sort of way. Handsome as a devil, sweet as one of Hill's sugary confections. And he smelled like a walk in the woods after the spring rain. Glorious!

He thought far too well of himself, but he had probably been told all his life how charming and perfect he was. Arrogant seemed like a good word for him. Prideful, certainly.

But he hadn't *seemed* dishonest. I always prided myself on judging characters, and I hadn't sensed that in him, though he *was* a thief. At least he admitted it. Ah, well, I had thought he had better sense than to go out and kiss Mildred Purvis, too. I wanted to spit the taste of his lips off of my own, but it was too late for that.

I had a stupid crush on a burglar.

Darcy

"THANK HEAVEN YOU'RE BACK so quickly! I need someone in his right mind."

My cousin, Colonel Richard Fitzwilliam, strolled into my study without even bothering to be announced. Dobbs had standing instructions just to let Richard pass, and my cousin took full advantage of the arrangement whenever it suited him.

I pushed aside the letter I had been trying—unsuccessfully—to write. "Richard. I thought you were at Rosings."

"Was, my good fellow. And still might have been, were it not for Lady Catherine's bad temper."

"How so? Tea?"

"I—yes, please—I nearly chased my poor carriage horses out of the drive just to get away from her. Egad, the woman is ambitious. Did you know she never even paid Elgin for that marble she got from him?"

I was in the midst of summoning Dobbs, but at that, I turned around, incredulous. "What? How?"

Richard shrugged. "She gave him a letter saying she would pay once it passed muster with Carruthers, but she never paid the man. Poor fellow is barely keeping a roof over his head, and she cheated him straight up. And got high and mighty with me when I called her on it."

"I shouldn't wonder. So that was why you left in such haste."

"No, as a matter of fact, it wasn't. She caught wind that Father is in league with a certain highness to cut her out of her little hobby, and she drove me out of Rosings for a spy."

I snorted. "Which is precisely what you were."

"Yes, but she did not have to toss my dinner goblet in my face. She's lucky she isn't a man, or else I'd... I say, is that what I think it is?"

I glanced over my shoulder at the vase sitting on the end table in the corner. "I purchased that yesterday. There is a merchant here in London by the name of Gardiner. The earl told me of him. When I went to see him and asked about certain antiquities, he showed me that."

Richard walked over to the vase and lifted it to look inside at the details of the clay. "Amphora. What do you think? Fifth century?"

I got up to follow him over to the vase. "It appears to be. Perhaps sixth."

He tilted it from all angles, testing its weight and balance and, as I had, examining the places where cracks had started. Some had been mended, while others looked to have started long after the vase had ended its useful life. The figures were exquisitely described in burnished detail, and it boasted ornate feathered handles on each side. It really was a magnificent example of the type.

It was a shame it was a fake.

"What is this?" Richard asked. He scraped his thumbnail over some of the Attic black paint at the bottom edge. It was ragged and worn and looked as though it would flake off, but it did not. He hefted its weight again, then set it down and squinted at me. "Darcy, you've been taken in!"

I smirked and chuckled. "No. I bought exactly what I wanted to buy. Beautiful, is it not?"

"Well, yes, but it's nearly worthless. It's an excellent copy, perhaps the best I've ever seen, but I hope you gave no more than five or ten pounds for it."

"I did not buy it for its aesthetic qualities. I was hoping to learn something, and I have."

"And what is that?"

I sighed and clucked my tongue. "No matter. Do you remember Charles Bingley at all?"

Richard strolled over to a chair and dropped into it, kicking his boots out and slouching like a schoolboy. He only ever did that when it was just the two of us. "Red-haired chap, isn't he? Son of a woolen miller from Northamptonshire."

"That's the fellow. I've taken up with him of late. He is an excellent sort, though somewhat accident-prone, and I've quite developed a liking for him. In fact, he has just secured an estate in Hertfordshire and has invited me to join him for some sport next week."

"Oh? That's fine, then. Friendly, unaffected lad like Bingley would be good for you."

I glanced at him narrowly. "What is that supposed to mean?"

Richard straightened as the tea cart appeared through the door. "It means you could use a few new associates who are not trying to get you for your purse, your social standing, or your advice."

"My advice is precisely what he desired."

"But Bingley would not be the chap to use you shamelessly. He would be your friend for life if you helped him for five minutes. Do you plan to go with him?"

I waited until the maid had poured the tea and excused herself before I replied. "I am trying to persuade myself against it."

"Whatever for? Have you anything better to do?"

Not getting entangled with that minx with the sparkling eyes seemed like a passing good scheme. Much as I wanted to. But I simply cleared my throat and changed the subject. "Have you spoken with your father?"

"Oh, yes. Just before I came here. I say, he's as bad as Lady Catherine, only he has more power. Kept going on and on about those marbles as if it were a matter of national import."

"Some say it is."

"Mmm." Richard sipped his tea. "He said you brokered a purchase for him on behalf of His Royal Highness in... I say, it was in Hertfordshire. Why, Darcy! How convenient. You really ought to go back with Bingley next week so you could help introduce him to the neighbors. He would kiss your feet."

"I have had enough kissing, thank you," I retorted testily.

Richard lowered his cup. "What is this?"

"Nothing."

"Bollocks! Since I came into the room, you have not carried on with a single conversation. You haven't even asked what tipped Lady Catherine off that I was not simply there to bask in her opulent presence. You're nearly red in the face, and you haven't stopped fidgeting since you sat down. Who is she?"

I gripped the armrests of my chair. "What tipped Lady Catherine off?"

"Oh, no. I am not letting you switch the conversation again. You are positively sweating! Why, you look just like you did when I made you hide in that closet under the stairwell at Matlock when we were boys."

I slid a finger under my cravat and wished he had not brought up that particular memory. I could still recall the closeness, the suffocating walls seeming to lean toward me in the darkness, the sensation of being trapped and altogether too warm, with no notion of where to find the secret door once Richard had closed it. "That was a bit of unfair bullying on your part," I protested.

"And you still have not forgiven me for it! But no matter, for I should very much like to learn what has you sweating now. If I were a betting man—which, I suppose, I am—I would lay money that you ran afoul of some Hertfordshire lass while you were there. What did she do, try to commit matrimony upon you? Or did you like her, but she did not return the sentiment?"

"Please. You do make everything so simplistic."

"Because it is. How did you meet her?"

I shook my head and got up to pace the room. "Who says there was a lady?"

"Your face says it. Come, Darcy, you never could get through a conversation with a lady without looking nearly faint afterward."

"Yes, well, it seems I managed it this time. I daren't encounter her again, or heaven help me."

"Heaven just might be helping you now, though you won't confess it."

I stopped at the window and stared out, trying to regulate my breath. Richard was right about one thing. I had not been easy since my first encounter with Elizabeth Bennet.

When I was with her, I could not help myself. She was like striking a flint to kindling, and before I knew what was happening, I was engulfed, with absolutely no desire to save myself.

But that was not what terrified me the most. The reason I was nearly shivering and my pulse was skittering was that when I was apart from her, I could not forget her. Those fine, laughing eyes, the breezy boldness with which she tossed all my false bravado back in my face. I could not close my eyes, but she filled my imagination.

How was that even possible? I had only encountered her a few times, and each time, she had the upper hand. Why, she ought to have every reason to think me an infamous criminal, a blackguard, and a scoundrel! Yet she had toyed with me. With no fear, she had baited me, teased me, and even consented to help me. Well... after she was the one who injured me in the first place. But she had not done it from spite.

I had been in jest when I'd asked her to sew me up after she struck me at Netherfield. Mostly. When did *I* ever tease a lady? Never! But at a time when I ought rightly to have been preoccupied with the royal business Lord Matlock had enlisted me for, all I could think of was what I would say if I saw her again.

Which was precisely why I should avoid her. Or marry her. I had not made my mind up which.

"Did the earl say when he meant to go to Hertfordshire?" I asked, my gaze still fixed out the window.

Richard tsked, and I heard him getting out of his chair. "You are simply determined not to tell me what has you all a-dither. Very well, I shall not ask again. To answer your question, he was not going to Hertfordshire himself."

I turned. "What?"

Richard swallowed the last of his tea and set the cup aside. "He said your word was good enough for him, and if you found the sculpture to be one of Elgin's smaller artifacts, His Royal Highness is prepared to send for it immediately. I think the prince's men left for Hertfordshire this afternoon."

An icy chill shot down my spine. "I thought the earl meant to inspect it personally! I told him he should. He only sent me in haste because he got word that Lady Catherine was trying to cut him out of it. I spoke with Mr. Bennet, he agreed to wait on Matlock to complete the transaction, and that was the end of it."

"What, you never saw it yourself?"

I swallowed and put a hand to my mouth. "Good heavens. No, it was not possible at the moment. But Lady Catherine's emissary saw it, and he was trying with all his might to secure it for her. Surely—"

"Collins would buy a painted rock if he thought Lady Catherine wanted it. The man is an idiot."

"Blast!" Blood was pounding in my ears, and all my vision blurred, save for one point. I stared at the letter I had been trying to compose, still sitting unfinished on my desk, as an chilling dread seized my heart. "The earl will not even have it brought to him in London first?"

"Why should he? According to you, it was everything Bennet claimed it was, and Prinny was impatient to see it."

I ground my teeth, and my fist still cupped over my chin as I growled an epithet. Or three. "Devil take me. I have to put a stop to the purchase!"

"I'm afraid it is too late for that, old boy. Egad, but you have turned from red in the face to positively green! What is the trouble?"

I rounded on him. "The prince could be buying a fake! If it is, and he finds it to be so, we are all ruined!"

Richard paled. "Darcy, tell me you are mistaken."

"I wish I were. That vase over there came from Mr. Bennet's 'collection.' I thought something seemed off, and that only confirmed my suspicions."

My cousin swallowed. "You have to fix this. I don't know how you're going to do it, but do something!"

I nodded and raced to the door. "Dobbs! Have my carriage brought round. I must leave for Hertfordshire within a quarter hour!"

Thirteen

Elizabeth

M<small>R. COLLINS WAS GROWING</small> more impatient by the hour. Papa continued to put him off, saying that he was considering not even selling the Eros statue, or at least that he would not be selling to the first person to offer. I continued to plead with him when we were in private not to sell it to Lady Catherine at all, and at last, he said he agreed with me.

But it was not until the fourth day of Mr. Collins' stay that Papa finally consented to see the man in his study. Jane and I shared a glance, and we both let go a sigh of relief. Surely, Papa would send him away now, having toyed with him long enough.

But, my father reasoned, Mr. Collins was the heir to Longbourn, so it was not altogether improper that the man should receive some hospitality in his future home, over and beyond his stated object of securing the sculpture. And Mama would not hear of him going until he had a chance to know her daughters—save for Jane—so that he might choose a bride from among us.

Not that any of us were interested in that scheme. I had caught Lydia and Kitty behind the house, giggling Mr. Collins' name and then pretending to cast up their accounts. Mary refused to make eye contact with him, and I had decided that I would rather sit beside Collins than opposite him at table because watching him eat revolted me. No, Mama would not find a willing daughter to become the next mistress of Longbourn.

And so, it was with a sense of deliverance that I watched Mr. Collins disappear inside the study. Mama and my sisters and I had just returned from shopping in Meryton, and I'd put a hole in my stocking on the way back. I settled down with my sewing basket to mend it and expected all would be right in half an hour. Collins would take his leave by the morrow, and life would resume as before.

Five minutes later, however, he was back. "Cousin Elizabeth, I wonder if I might have a word?"

The stocking fell into my lap. Jane's eyes found mine with a fresh horror, and she shook her head ever so subtly.

"Of course she will!" Mama answered for me. "Jane, I want you upstairs. And you, too, Kitty. Come! I need to speak with you about something!"

Collins stood in the middle of the doorway while everyone tried to crowd past him. He didn't even think to move out of the way—just stared at them as they squeezed out. Then he smoothed back the long hair he'd combed over his balding spot, walked up to me, and hit the rug.

"Dearest cousin Elizabeth! I know not when the fancy overtook me, but it has been many moments that I have considered you the handsomest woman of my acquaintance!" He grabbed my hand right out of my lap and kissed the backs of my fingers.

I pulled my hand away, but I could not stand up because he was blocking my escape. "Mr. Collins! You forget yourself."

"Oh, but I have not, my dear cousin! Perhaps you will allow me to delineate my reasons for marrying. First, Lady Catherine has described the ideal course for a parson as that of a head of his household, marrying prudently, that all decorum should be served and I might gain for myself a modest and reliable helpmeet. Second, I believe it is the duty of a parson to set the example of felicity—"

"Mr. Collins, forgive me for interrupting, but you could not prevail upon me with any reason whatsoever, for I do not intend to accept."

He drew a shaking breath, his eyes bulging, and reached for my hand once more. "And lastly, it is the express desire of Lady Catherine that I ought to secure, by purchase or marriage or any means necessary, that upon which her heart is set."

I blinked. Shook my head. "You want to marry me just so you can buy the statue for Lady Catherine? I have never heard anything so absurd!"

"Not merely to please Lady Catherine, but ourselves! It occurs to me that in the sad but inevitable future, your father's decease may create such a hardship that is in my power to alleviate. My dearest cousin, allow me to protest the earnestness of my suit, the depth of my feelings—"

I lurched to my feet, heedless that I bumped him in the chin with my knee. "Feelings which cannot have existed for more than five minutes! Mr. Collins, I have had quite enough. I must insist that you respect my refusal. It is not possible for me to accept."

Still squatting on the floor, he spun to face me as I stepped around him. "But Miss Elizabeth! Lady Catherine will be most seriously displeased!"

I marched out of the room, leaving his complaints and blatherings behind, and burst through the door of my father's study. "Papa! You cannot imagine what that oaf has done now!"

Papa was just dipping his quill in the inkpot, but he looked up with a bemused smile. "I expect he has taken it into his head to try marrying one of my daughters. Was it Lydia?"

I crossed my arms and huffed. "This is no laughing matter! He actually plopped down in front of me and asked for my hand in marriage, and do you know why? Because he wants that cursed statue!"

"Elizabeth, my child, language. What answer did you give him?"

I snorted. "Of course I refused him!"

He nodded, his eyes on the paper before him. "Excellent, excellent. 'Twould be very awkward if you accepted."

"Awkward does not begin to describe my feelings on the matter. The man is a toad."

"Hmm? Oh! Yes, I would think you could do far better than Collins, but I was thinking of the sculpture. I'm afraid Lady Catherine cannot get it for love or money at this point."

I sighed and felt my racing heart slow. "Oh, Papa, I am so glad to hear it. It was not worth whatever risk—"

"What I mean is that I have accepted a better offer." He squinted at his paper, then shook his head, his eyebrows jumping. "A *far* better offer."

My stomach dropped into my shoes. "Papa, what have you done?" I whispered.

"Done? Why, I have provided five hundred pounds more for your dowries and a vast deal of amusement for myself." He dipped his pen again. "I hear that Lady Catherine will be 'displeased.' So much the better. What good are competing buyers if one is not snubbed in the end?"

I rocked forward and braced my knuckles on his desk. "To *whom* did you sell it?"

"Well, he outranks a baronet's widow," Papa chuckled.

I closed my eyes. It wouldn't do any good to pray this wasn't happening. "Tell me it was not some earl."

"Oh, an earl brokered the transaction, to be sure. As a matter of fact, even the Earl of Matlock acted through an agent—someone called Darcy. I suppose that tells us where we rank in the food chain, doesn't it? There must be at least two steps of separation between us and our future king."

My knees buckled.

"Lizzy!" Papa shot up from his chair to peer at me over his desk. "Did you get too much sun on your outing?"

I pushed myself up from the floor, still shaking and dizzy, and I felt cautiously for the front of his desk to pull myself upright. "Papa, you did not say what I think you just said. You are not selling that thing to the Prince Regent! Tell me I misheard!"

"Why, no, I believe you heard me aright. A handsome price he paid, too—or will pay, once he is satisfied with it. I'm to receive payment after it is delivered, and such a payment it is! But there, he is royalty, and I warrant he is always obliged to pay more than double whenever he chases his little whims. Shall I have Hill bring you something?"

"No! Oh, Papa, you cannot sell that to *anyone*, least of all royalty! Only think what will be made of it if he learns what it is—or, rather, what it is *not*. Prince or no prince, you simply must call off the sale!"

Papa chuckled. "It is too late for that, my dear. His Highness already sent his men to collect it. Why do you think I made certain to send everyone to town?"

"You..." I twirled around, and indeed, the statue was no longer on the pedestal in the corner of his study. I stared at the empty surface, willing it to reappear. "It's gone," was all I could manage.

"Indeed, and now I have some correspondence to attend with Gardiner and Philips. If you would be so kind, Elizabeth, I mean to finish my letter before the ink dries in my pot."

I just blinked, still staring. "It's gone. You sold it to the p... the pr..." My breath was coming in short, unhelpful strangles, and I couldn't see clearly.

"Now, Elizabeth, I must beg you not to tell your mother that bit of information. What peace would I have then? Heavens! She will want to know when we are invited to the palace for a royal ball. Do kindly let me finish my letter in peace." He put his hand on my shoulder and guided me to the door, then closed it behind me.

What to do? Papa had signed his own warrant! He knew better than I that the Eros statue was not one of Elgin's, and it was only a matter of time before someone noticed. How could he think he could keep up the deception? The Prince Regent and his art scholars simply must not be allowed to see it! But how?

An idea tickled the back of my mind. A stupid idea, but in desperate times, it is never the brilliant ideas that present themselves. I needed help, and there was only one person I could turn to.

I didn't know how to find him. I didn't even know where to start, save that he was not sitting in Longbourn's drawing room beside Collins. I pulled on my pelisse, jerked my bonnet knot tight under my chin, and burst through the door outside.

Directly into his arms.

Darcy

"Y OU DO HAVE SUCH a way of coming up on me. Do you ever walk mildly into a room, or is it always this crash and thunder with you?"

Elizabeth Bennet stiffened and pushed away—much to my regret—shoving against my chest with one hand and righting her skewed bonnet with the other. "To be more precise, I am not coming *into* a room just now but leaving one."

"And in a fearful rush, too. Dare I ask who has offended you this time?"

Her lips tightened, and her eyes flashed. "Steal any more spoons lately?"

"What?"

"You heard me. How does your new greatcoat suit you?"

I shook my head. "You are speaking in riddles, Miss Bennet. I am afraid I have no time for such games."

She was grinding her teeth, her nostrils fluttering in contempt—for what, I knew not—but she drank in a deep breath, and her shoulders dropped. "Neither do I. You are a terrible person, but it seems I am in need of a terrible person just now."

I removed my hat. "For you, Miss Bennet, I believe I could even be a horrible person. Perhaps even an appalling one. What is the trouble?"

She glanced over her shoulder at the house. "Not here."

I replaced my hat and extended my arm for her to take. "Very well. Let us slip quietly into the forest, that none shall be the wiser."

Elizabeth narrowed her eyes. "I do not know what your word is worth, but can I trust you, sir?"

"Miss Bennet, I will guard you like you were my own sister. You may depend on it."

"Hah! I already know that for a falsehood."

"Not at all." She wasn't taking my arm, so I clasped her hand and gently tugged her forward. "No harm ever befell my sister when I was present, and so far, *I* have been the only one injured when you and I are in company. I ought instead to be asking for assurance from you that you will refrain from wounding me."

She clamped her teeth into her lower lip, and her eyes fluttered closed in a long-suffering sigh. "I cannot believe I am doing this."

E LIZABETH LED ME TO the cow barn and, after looking inside to be certain we were alone, proceeded to climb the ladder up to the hayloft. Was she... serious? That was not the sort of business I had in mind.

"Are you coming?" she asked when she gained the top. I still had not set my foot on the rung because I was so consumed with watching her. Was it hot in that barn? I seemed to be having some trouble breathing.

This was over my head. I'd only come to Longbourn to ask a few questions, and now I was climbing into a hayloft with the only woman who ever made me lose track of my brain. I would be lucky if I came back down with my sanity intact.

But there was nothing else for it, so I tested the ladder and carefully made my way up.

She had already settled herself in a sort of nest amid the loose hay; her crossed arms resting on her knees. The toes of her shoes peeped from under her skirts, and she was waiting for me with a satirical smile.

"Don't tell me you have never climbed a ladder before. I thought that was one of the tools of your trade."

"Only when necessary." I ducked under the low roof, removing my hat and searching for a place to sit. The hay was mounded in such a way that there was nowhere to sit that did not leave me almost touching her. Exactly what I'd been afraid of.

"Why are you even here?"

I shuffled my seat a little more deeply into the hay. "Perhaps it is best if you go first. My errand will not be quick to explain."

"Very well. There is a... a thing. I need it back."

I folded my hands on my knee. "Perhaps you would care to elaborate."

She rolled her eyes and blew out a sigh. "A sculpture. It is about this high—" she held her hand roughly eighteen inches above the hay floor—"and made of marble. My father has sold it to... well, to someone, and now I need someone of your..." She swept those dark eyes over me, head to toe. "Expertise."

"What expertise is that? So far, the only thing you know for a certainty that I can do is—"

"I do not need to be kissed."

I stopped, and a slow grin overtook my face. I couldn't help it. Heaven have mercy, but she was delicious. "More is the pity."

"Well, that seems to be what you do best," she snapped. "Have you any other talents, or are you all a sham?"

"Lest we forget, the second time, *you* were the one who kissed *me*."

She examined her fingernails. "I was only exploiting a weakness, and it worked."

"It was a pleasant distraction, I'll admit, but I did not entirely forget the reason I came to speak with you. Nor have I now."

"Right. So, can you do it, or can't you?"

"Do what? You've told me nothing except there is a statue, and you think me a talented kisser."

Her cheeks flamed. "I did not say that."

I grinned. I might be in the middle of the worst crisis ever to tarnish my family's name. But there in the dusky loft, with the air balmy and our voices muted to intimate whispers, all thoughts of sculptures and scandals faded. I was staring fixedly at her plump, sweet lips, my breath coming in shallow bursts and my core buzzing as if I had had too much wine.

"You said," I reminded her, "that it was my particular expertise. Have you many examples to compare me to?"

She sighed. "You really are insufferable."

"Indeed, but you have answered none of my questions."

Elizabeth's lips thinned. "Perhaps one or two, but from what I gather, you are the true proficient. Heaven and earth! How many ladies have you beguiled?"

"Apparently, none. Very well, Miss Bennet. What do you want me to do about this statue? You say it is gone already?"

She nodded, her eyes seeming to grow larger. "My father has sold it, and he does not seem to understand the fearful trouble he has caused... is causing... what *could* happen." She huffed and stared at her feet. When she spoke again, it was in a broken whisper. "I tried to stop him, to keep him from ruining us all, but I am too late!"

"Here, now." I pulled my handkerchief out and offered it to her. She shook her head at first, then seized it and buried her face in it.

I would never wash it again.

The most unfair thing in the world is when a woman cries. On my honor, there is nothing to make a man feel more helpless and more desperate to do something about it. I glanced about as if there might be something else I could offer her in that musty loft. Something to comfort her, put things right. But all I could give was my voice, uncertain and cracked as it was.

"Come..." I cleared my throat when my voice broke. "Come, Miss Bennet, let us speak rationally. You say your father sold this sculpture? Was it the one I asked you about... ah... when I approached you in the wood?"

Her shoulders were shaking, and she nodded.

The turbulent terror that had been burning my chest since London flamed brighter. It must be as I had feared, and the Bennets were not the only family that would be ruined by this imbroglio. But I needed to hear it from her lips, to be sure.

I leaned forward, my face only inches from hers. "And why should his selling it trouble you so?"

She did not answer. She lifted her face once, opened her mouth as if to speak, then her expression crumpled, and she wadded my handkerchief against her eyes. She was trembling from head to foot.

I ground my teeth and glared through the small window in the hayloft toward Longbourn house. Mr. Bennet was a fool. An amiable, amusing fool, perhaps even a well-meaning one, but his carelessness and arrogance could well be the undoing of us all.

And most unforgivably of all, he had made Elizabeth cry.

"Miss Bennet," I said, gently as I could, "tell me everything you know. What sort of sculpture is this? Where did it come from?"

She sucked in a long gulp of air and sniffed a few times, trying to compose herself. "Dare I tell you the truth?"

"If you do not, I cannot help you."

Her face turned up to me, her dark eyes luminous with feeling. "But if I tell you, you would have no reason to help me."

I took the wadded handkerchief from her fingers and boldly dabbed her cheek with it. I had to feel like I was doing *something*. "I have more reason than you can imagine."

Her lashes fluttered, her gaze fixed on my face. She drew herself up and let out a breath. "I suppose I have nothing to lose at this point."

"That remains to be seen. To whom did your father sell this?"

She wetted her lips. "Ah... someone... powerful."

I raised a brow. "And?"

"And... ah... It's not... well, what I mean is that it's not exactly... ah..."

"It's a fake, isn't it?"

She blinked. Swallowed. Then she dipped her head and nodded, swiping her cheek with the heel of her hand. "How did you guess?"

"Never mind that now. I suppose you want to call off this powerful person's purchase of the sculpture. Is that right?"

"But it is too late for that! It has already been collected and is on its way to London, even now!"

I chewed on that for a moment. "There must be some way to reason with His... I mean, with this buyer. We send a letter, speak with the earl—or someone. We declare it a mistake, that is all."

"And my father is still ruined, and the rest of us along with him!"

I gazed at her—the urgency in her posture, the pleading in her eyes... and I buckled. She wasn't coming to Fitzwilliam Darcy of Pemberley for help. She was asking William, the man she'd kissed in the woods. And I liked being William for her.

"So, what do you want to do instead?"

Fourteen

Elizabeth

"**S**TEAL IT!"

William—if that really was his name—lurched backward and toppled over into a loose pile of hay.

"Hush, or we will be overheard!" I leaned forward and scraped a lump of hay out of his face, and he sat up, spitting and sputtering and trying to dust his jacket off.

"To the devil with being overheard. We will be horsewhipped! And then hanged! Do you honestly—"

I clapped a hand over his mouth, pressing him back. "Shh!"

He blinked, his eyes sliding back and forth, and then he squinted. "Whuff?" he asked against my hand.

"Don't you hear them?" I looked over my shoulder. "My sisters are outside, somewhere nearby. If I take my hand off your mouth, you have to promise to be quiet." Carefully, I released him, holding his stare all the while to be certain he did nothing stupid.

"This is preposterous. Do you really think—"

I silenced him again, grabbing the back of his head with my other hand this time. I enjoyed it when he winced. "You really don't know when to be quiet, do you? The last thing we need is for my sister Lydia to find us up here! Can you *please* grow some common sense?"

He narrowed his eyes. Then he did something that made me blush to the roots of my hair. I felt his lips smiling under my palm... and then he kissed it. Open-mouthed and everything.

I reeled back, wiping my hand on my skirts. "Disgusting! For pity's sake, are you five years old?"

"I'm not the one who suggested stealing from someone so powerful you refused to name them!" he hissed. "What can you possibly be thinking?"

I scowled at him and put my finger up to go to the window. To my relief, Lydia and Kitty were cavorting across the yard in the other direction. "I am thinking it would be better for a thief to slip away with his prize and never be caught than for a respectable family with five poorly dowered daughters to live forever in disgrace! For myself, I could survive, but Jane is too good. I cannot bear to think of what would become of them all when my father can no longer support us."

"Yes, well, suppose this thief *is* caught? What then?"

I smiled. "You haven't been caught yet. Any luck selling those spoons?"

He growled and rolled his eyes. "I believe you must be operating under some grave misconceptions."

"And I'm really not interested in hearing all the mitigating circumstances you probably want to claim. What I want to know is, will you do it?"

He crossed his arms, which was probably meant to look forbidding. But he had hay sticking at odd angles out of his hair, and the buttons of his jacket had popped open to reveal a... rather muscular chest. He looked not in the least menacing. Rather, he was somewhere between absurd and mouth-watering. "No."

"But think of it! You already asked about this sculpture, so you must know something about it. You could demand a fine price for it!"

He cocked his head, staring in disbelief. "You have some peculiar notions of my character, Miss Bennet."

"And they are not unfounded. I have never yet seen you do anything 'normal.' Pinching vases or sneaking up behind people in the woods? You are no gentleman, sir, however much you may protest. And it seems that not being a gentleman has paid rather well for you, as I see you have yet another custom-tailored jacket. You may have stolen Mr. Purvis's great-coat, but this one has been made to fit you by a master."

He squared his shoulders and glanced self-consciously down at that jacket. "I suppose it would do me little good to set right certain facts."

"I do have several questions. Who are you, really?"

He sighed, and his jaw shifted as he gazed at me narrowly. "That is not the real question."

"Excuse me, but I think I know very well what my real question is. What is your name?"

The side of his mouth tugged upward. "I told you. William."

"The rest of it."

"*Fitz*william."

I scowled and shook my head. "If you cannot at least answer a simple question seriously..."

"That *is* my name."

"And who gave it to you? Who are your people? Where do you come from?"

He shifted against the hay pile as if he were just getting comfortable. "Miss Bennet, you just asked me to steal something which does not belong to me and no longer belongs to you. Why this fuss about my origins when you are suggesting something immoral and illegal?"

"You are a fine one to talk." I picked some straw off my skirts. "And it is not precisely 'not mine anymore.' Payment was not to be remitted until the P... the sculpture was received. I only want to prevent it from being received."

"And where is it going? How long ago was it taken away?"

I swallowed. "Early this afternoon. I... I don't know where it is going."

"And yet you want me to track it down and steal it!"

"Quiet!" I put my hand up and looked back at the window. Lydia and Kitty's voices had returned. "Will you please stop shouting? I'll end up stuck with you if my mother ever finds out we were alone up here."

His mouth twitched into a vague smile. "That fate might not be as dismal as you fear."

"For you! I don't even know your name!"

His smile grew wider. "Now you're the one making the most noise."

I bit back a huff of frustration. "I despise you."

"Compliments will get you nowhere, Miss Bennet. Come, I must have some information to work from, if we are to salvage this situation for all concerned. You said it went to London. Have you anyone you know in London?"

I sat back on the straw. "My uncle Gardiner. He is a merchant in Cheapside."

He nodded. "I know of this man."

I snorted. "How? Uncle Gardiner has never done an illegal thing in his life. Not knowingly, anyway."

"I make it my business to know all manner of people. Now suppose I go to this Gardiner fellow and speak with one or two other people of my acquaintance, and we see if we can get this whole affair straightened out?"

"Oh, no, you cannot involve my uncle!" I pleaded. "He was not involved in this transaction, and if he learned it was a f..." I drew a breath.

"A fake?"

"Yes, that. If he knew, he would start to question everything. He would never be easy again! He is innocent of any wrongdoing. I cannot have that on his conscience, please!"

Something in William's face shifted. It was as if a hardness in him softened, his annoyance bleeding out a little. He studied me for a few seconds, saying nothing, then shook his head and waved his hand. "Very well. We do not involve Mr. Gardiner. But how am I to know how to proceed? I cannot very well ride back and forth to London every time I must speak with someone."

"I'll go to London," I blurted before I could think.

"And do what?"

"I'll..." I chewed my lip. "I'll ask my aunt if I might come for a visit. Mama would not object. I could stay in Cheapside, and you could reach me there."

"And what good would that do me? To be of any use to me, you would have to be with me. I don't even know what this thing is supposed to look like."

I gasped. "*With* you? How on earth would we manage that?"

"You will simply have to think of something. Obviously, we cannot reason with your father, and you do not wish me to involve Mr. Gardiner."

"But I cannot walk around London with you unchaperoned! My aunt is kindness itself, but even she would forbid it!"

"Do you have any sensible sisters? Even one?"

I wanted to slap him. Or split his head open again. "Jane," I grumbled. "She is everything good and sweet and rational. But you won't get Mama to let her go to London now because she has got it in her head that Jane has to marry our new neighbor. We haven't even met him! He could have bad breath and leprosy, but Mama is determined to ensnare the poor man. Someone named Bingley."

William's eyes twinkled in the dusky light from the hayloft window. "What if I told you that there may be a way for your mother to have her heart's desire in London?"

I straightened. "I'm listening."

Darcy

I T WAS THE STUPIDEST idea I had ever had. *Why* would I be so brainless as to agree to any of this? How the devil was I to get back this worthless statue when it had already been collected by the prince's men? It would be under guard on the road and under guard once it reached the palace.

But it was also bloody difficult to say no to Elizabeth Bennet. And that was going to create a serious problem for me one day.

She left me stowed in the barn like a stray dog while she went to the house to arrange her journey to London. If she could persuade Mrs. Bennet, that was the end of all arguments. I would be committed. I squeezed my eyes shut and prayed she would fail.

Ten minutes later, she returned, and her face said all. "Mama has agreed!"

I sighed and bade farewell to my life as I had known it. "Very well. What day do you travel?"

"I am afraid you do not understand the urgency of our situation. Every moment wasted is one that might mean disaster. We may not be in time to prevent the sculpture from arriving, but once it is seen by whoever is designated to receive and inspect it, all hope is lost. We must go this very hour."

"Without even writing to your relatives in London to request the honor of visiting?"

She grinned. "As for that, Papa usually 'forgets' to post letters about our trips to London. Our dear aunt is a saint among women, and she has assured Jane and me that we are welcome anytime, day or night, because she is so used to us turning up without warning."

"Your aunt is kinder than most."

"She is. Jane is packing her trunk, and we are to take the post from the Meryton Inn. We ought to be just in time."

"The post! Here, I cannot let two ladies ride post when I have a perfectly good carriage waiting at the inn."

She cocked a wary eye at me. "A thief who has his own carriage? Who *are* you?"

"Not the man you would expect to be tangled in this disaster."

Elizabeth nodded, her gaze still skeptical. "Nothing about you adds up, sir."

"I expect not. When will you and your sister be ready to depart?"

"I need a quarter of an hour. My father gave orders for the buggy to be hitched up, and it will take us to town."

"I will meet you at the inn." I reached for my hat and frowned in dismay when I found it covered in straw. I was dusty and disheveled from boots to cravat.

"I know that expression. You are wondering how you will show your face in public, looking as you are. You just put one foot in front of the other. See?" She held her arms aloft and pantomimed walking.

I glared at her. "You are very cheeky, Miss Bennet."

"I am only repeating what someone else once told me. You would be surprised how uncurious people really are."

"I look like a farmhand."

"You may look like many things, but a farmhand is not one of them." She patted my cheek with a teasing smile and started for the ladder.

I put my hand to the spot she had touched and found it rather warm. Hang it all. I was blushing like a schoolboy. "Wait. Where do I meet you?"

She stopped on the rung, her face turned up to me. A shaft of dusty light from the window broke over her features, bathing her skin, so she looked like a shabby sort of angel. And suddenly, I had to cough.

"In Cheapside, of course. I have no intention of riding in your carriage with you. What would people say?"

"You want to become a thief, but you're worried about what people will say? Perhaps you are not cut out for this, Miss Bennet."

She set her jaw and flicked her skirts back from her feet, her eyes still glittering up at me. "I will find my courage. I hope to heaven you have some of your own." She lowered her face then and climbed the rest of the way down.

I went to the window and waited until she had gone. She paused in the yard for a moment, gathering her younger sisters and shepherding them into the house. That was probably for my benefit, so I watched until the door closed and made my escape. The next time I would see her would be in London.

This was a stupid idea.

"**D**ARCY, I GOT YOUR note. What's so urgent that I had to leave off drinks at the club? Egad, is that straw in your hair?"

I brushed Richard's hand away from my face. "Never mind that. We have a rather serious problem, and I've not the least idea how to go about solving it."

Richard staked out a chair and made himself comfortable, then took in my appearance with a cynical grin. "What happened to you? Tumble in the hayloft with a handsome young—"

"That will be quite enough. I've just come from Hertfordshire."

"But you only left this morning. You could have only been there long enough to change horses before you galloped back."

"I was there somewhat longer than that. Long enough to discover the true nature of the situation. Richard, the statue is *not* one from Elgin's collection. I do not know precisely what it is, but it is not what Mr. Bennet claimed or what the Prince of Wales thinks he purchased."

He swallowed and put a hand to his mouth. "I was afraid of that. What do you mean to do?"

I walked to the decanter to pour some ablution over my crazed and addled brain, and then I poured a second glass for my cousin. "We have to get it back. The trouble is, it had already left Longbourn by the time I arrived, and I do not know where it has been taken. I do not even know what it looks like."

"I can help you with the first. Father said it is going to the Royal Academy—Somerset House—before he moves it to his royal residence."

"Where it will no doubt be investigated and inspected by every sculptor in the Academy." I swallowed some of my drink. "But at least it is not going to Carlton House straightaway. What else do you know?"

"Very little. It will be a day or two at least before anyone gets round to looking it over. Prinny is in Scotland at the moment, entertaining himself with a new mistress, they say."

"There is another mercy. I do not need to contend with him or the royal guard. What else do you know?"

Richard's brow creased, and he put a finger to his lips and shook his head. "Not much. Oh, but you will never guess who I encountered outside the club, trying to buy his way in."

I waved carelessly as I paced by him. "I don't know. George Wickham."

"Spot on!"

I stopped. "That was a wild guess."

"But correct, nonetheless."

I sipped again from my glass. Wickham was the son of my father's steward—and the one who had taught me to pick locks and climb through windows when I was a boy. I had not seen him and scarcely heard his name since the reading of my father's will five years previously, when he received the living set aside for him and vanished. "Wickham is in London?"

"He is, and he spent all his money. Again."

"Tell me something that would surprise me."

"Well, he looked to be intoxicated."

"Try again."

"And he was wearing an enormous coat, too large for him, with about a dozen silver spoons filling some pockets he had sewn into the lining. He took me aside and showed them to me, trying to get me to buy them off him."

I halted, my neck prickling. "Spoons? And a coat too large for him?"

Richard laughed and shook his head. "Two guesses about what the old boy has been up to."

"I know exactly what he's been up to and where he's been doing it. Do you know where he is now?"

"Oh, yes. He is rooming with some doxy over in the St. Giles Rookery. Asked about you, though."

I raised my brows. "How much money does he want?"

"More than you want to give him. I told him to bugger off."

I walked to the window to stare outside. The streets were already dark, with lanterns glowing along the walks. There would be no meeting with Elizabeth Bennet tonight. Tomorrow, we would test our destiny. Tomorrow, we would save both our families, or we would be ruined together.

But perhaps there was a way to increase our chances of success... and see a bit of justice done along the way. "I need to speak with Wickham," I mumbled.

"Wickham! What the devil for?"

I turned back to Richard. "I just had an idea."

FIFTEEN

Elizabeth

"I THANK YOU FOR the offer, Aunt, but the carriage is unnecessary. Jane's beau has offered to escort us to Bond Street himself."

Aunt Gardiner gave me a dubious look over her tea. "Forgive me for saying, Lizzy, but this is all rather sudden. How did she meet this Mr. Bingley?"

I focused my attention on my poached egg because I was a terrible liar. "He is to be our new neighbor. Uncle Philips knows him." There. That was all true.

"Indeed! I say, dear Jane has captured him rather quickly. Your mother must be pleased. Is he amiable?"

I cleared my throat. "Oh-oh, yes. Yes, I think him rather amiable. I suppose."

"Well, that is... that is wonderful. Does Jane truly like him? I would not wish to see her accept someone so quickly just to please others."

I swallowed my dry toast and tried to think of some truthful response. "I know no harm of him, Aunt. I have been assured that he is gentlemanly in every way." Though I still wondered how well I could trust the assessment of a burglar.

Aunt Gardiner shook her head. "You young ladies do things in such a fearful headlong rush these days. Are you certain you do not need me to attend you? Your father really believes Jane will be safe with only you and his sister as her chaperons?"

"I am confident. Moreover, I understand Mr. Bingley is a rather modest man, and you know Jane. I think too much company would make them uncomfortable."

She sighed and surrendered. "How long do you plan to be away this afternoon?"

"Oh, did I not say? Mr. Bingley is coming by ten, and Jane is expected to ah... to take tea with his sisters before attending a play this evening. I am afraid we may be rather late."

My aunt's brow furrowed. "With such haste during their courtship, are we to expect a wedding within the fortnight? How long ago was this arranged? And how very like your father to neglect to tell us."

I shrugged and smiled weakly. "Yes, Papa can be forgetful. And as for a courtship, it is only a shopping outing and tea. Mama desired for Jane to have a new gown before the next ball, and Papa, for once, was happy to oblige. So long as he did not have to escort her."

"That sounds like him. Oh, my goodness, look at the hour. I will be wanted in the nursery, and you ought to be going upstairs to dress for your outing. I am looking forward to meeting this Mr. Bingley you praise so highly."

She rose and left me alone in the room. I let out a groan and rolled my eyes to the ceiling. "I'm looking forward to meeting him, too."

Darcy

"I SAY, DARCY, I never thought to hear from you again." George Wickham strolled confidently into my study, flanked by Richard, who was regarding him with a scowl and watching Wickham's hands like a hawk. He'd already made certain that nothing small and valuable remained within arm's length of Wickham's path through the room.

I nodded curtly. "You are looking well, George. Do be seated. Sherry?"

He smiled. "I don't mind if I do."

I poured and waited for Wickham to relax in his seat, sniffing the glass as if he relished the very aroma.

"Only the best, eh, Darcy?" He sipped, his eyes closed, and drank in a long sigh. "Now, then, I know this is only a ploy to soften me up a bit, but it is having the proper effect. You must need something that you cannot or will not do for yourself."

I met Richard's gaze. He still disapproved of this idea, but not on moral or legal grounds. He just didn't trust Wickham.

I topped off Wickham's glass. "I understand you have been keeping busy lately."

Wickham chuckled and sipped. "I didn't know you were keeping tabs on me. I suppose I ought not to be surprised."

"I had a passing interest. You've been spending a bit of time in Hertfordshire this past month. Stealing spoons and seducing ladies?"

He coughed and cleared his throat. "Egad, Darcy. I didn't know you'd had me followed. Who was your informant?" He shot a hard glare at Richard.

My cousin held up his hands. "Don't look at me. I was in Kent."

"Then who was it? No! I know you won't tell me. And you're not set to turn me in, or you would not have invited me here to ply me with your best sherry."

"Perspicacious as ever." I folded my hands on my desk. "Let us simply work forward with the assumption that I can and will have you imprisoned on the strength of witness testimonies. If need be."

Wickham rolled his eyes and set the glass on my desk with a clunk. "Carrot and stick. Very well, Darcy. What do you want?"

I glanced at Richard, then smiled at Wickham. "*That* is the proper question."

Wickham looked nervously at my cousin, who had worn his military regalia today—brass buttons polished, medals glimmering. He gulped, then pointed. "Tell me I'm not working with *him*."

"Oh, believe me. I hate this as much as you do," Richard growled.

I lifted my hands in a helpless gesture. "He means to scare you straight."

Wickham reclaimed his glass and swallowed it in one slosh. "Consider me properly frightened. May I go now?"

"You certainly may," Richard said. "Our carriage is right outside."

Wickham blinked, first at Richard, then at me. "Am I not to know what is going on?"

I laughed. Dash it all, but I was enjoying having the upper hand on Wickham for a change. "Oh, you'll find out soon enough. I only want to be assured of your cooperation. However, I have another appointment to keep as well." I stood and pulled out my pocket watch, and, as if on cue, Dobbs opened the door of the study.

"Mr. Bingley is here, sir."

I nodded. "Show him in, please. We are finished here." I came around the desk to face Wickham. "Safe journey, George. I shall see you back tomorrow, provided you are successful."

He turned a bewildered look on Richard, who had closed in behind him. "Suppose I'm not successful? I don't even know what I'm doing! What if I don't manage whatever you're asking?"

I shrugged and grinned. "I suppose you'll hang, after all, but I cannot be sure. I had not thought that far ahead."

His face crumpled into a sullen glare. "You really can be rather dark, Darcy."

I only smiled as Richard pushed him out the door.

B INGLEY STARED AT ME as if I had grown another eye in the middle of my forehead. "You have arranged what? Who is this lady?"

I stood for Dobbs to slide my coat up my shoulders, then reached for my hat. I was still rather careful about how I put my hat on, and I took a few extra seconds about it. "From what I am told—and my source is both reliable and forthright—the sweetest and most beautiful lady in all Hertfordshire. One of your new neighbors, as a matter of fact. She is here in London for a few days, and I understand she requires an escort."

"But why me? And how did you come to know her?"

"Oh, that? Simple, really. I had business there, and that business brought me into contact with the Bennet family of Longbourn."

"Bennet? Oh, indeed!" His eyes brightened. "My solicitor, Philips, told me the Bennet ladies were his nieces. He claimed they were the handsomest girls within fifty miles, but I assumed that was merely obligate praise for his relations."

"The praise was not unfounded. Now, look, Bingley, my business is not entirely concluded, which is why they are come to London. One of the Bennet ladies, Miss Elizabeth, is... Perhaps I ought to say she came on her father's behalf, and we require some chaperonage. I can think of no one more suitable to escort Miss Jane Bennet on a pleasant outing. There, will that suit?"

Bingley's face split into a wide grin. "Well, why did you not simply say so? Naturally, I would be delighted to! And what a happy coincidence that I am to take up residence in her neighborhood."

We stepped into his carriage, and I waited for the door to close. "Just one more thing. Miss Elizabeth insists on calling me 'William.' It is a... peculiarity of hers. I would just as soon you did not correct her."

Bingley gaped at me. "What?"

I smiled. "She is a unique sort of woman."

He just stared, his face still blank. Then inspiration flickered, and he laughed, slapping his knee. "You fancy her!"

"Nothing of the kind. I simply find her... fascinating."

"Ah. Yes. Fascinating. That is a long way from an infatuation."

I straightened my shoulders inside my coat and settled farther back in the seat. "Indeed. A very long way."

Elizabeth

J ANE NEVER COULD HIDE a blush. And right now, she was blushing more brightly than one of Mama's big showy rose bushes.

Mr. Bingley, if possible, was even redder than she. From his ruddy hair to his crimson cheeks, he looked flustered and abashed the moment his eyes found Jane. He doffed his hat, accidentally dropped his walking stick, and collided with his friend, the burglar, in his haste to bow.

"Miss Bennet! It is such an honor... I say, the pleasure is all mine, to be sure," he gushed. "I cannot tell you how delighted I was when D... when my friend here offered to introduce me to you." He straightened, a besotted smile already softening that freckled face. "I have heard much of you, Miss Bennet, but none of the praise did you justice."

I flicked a brow at Jane, my lips puckered into a little *I-told-you-so*. Her fingertips covered her lips, but she was grinning like Lydia when she has got into the sweets. "Oh, my," she whispered to me. "He is adorable!"

"May I?" He extended his arm, and Jane hooked her elbow through his. And then they just stared at each other with silly, blank looks and dreamy gazes.

My burglar had sidled up to me, and he lifted his chin toward the oblivious couple. "There. Do you feel safe letting him escort your sister?" he asked in a low voice.

I chuckled. "I think he might be even more harmless than she is."

William offered me his arm, and we followed Jane and Mr. Bingley down the steps. "I thought you would approve. They will do well enough, provided he does not trip her."

"What is that?"

"Bingley is the sort whose heart runs on before his head. If you look closely, you will see the remains of a bruise around his eyes and nose."

"I didn't have to look that closely, actually. Did he fall and break his nose?"

William grunted. "I will tell you how he got that some other time. But dropping his walking stick in his haste to bow to your sister is rather typical of his character. I say, you did not exaggerate when you claimed her to be the most beautiful of your family."

I slugged him playfully in the arm. "It is a good thing *we* are not courting, or I would have tossed you out on your ear for offending me just now."

His mouth turned up, and he patted my gloved hand. "Beauty is as beauty does. For myself, I rather fancy the feisty sort that keeps me on my toes. But as you say, we are not courting, and neither are they at present. It is only an outing."

I leaned closer with a whisper. "I should say they are already considering it more than an outing. You might just be setting your friend up for an inevitable marriage into a family that can provide no dowry, almost no social standing, and could be ruined tomorrow if our task fails."

He glanced at Mr. Bingley and Jane again. They were settled in the carriage already, giggling and speaking in low voices with their faces only inches apart. "Then we must see that our task does not fail."

Sixteen

Elizabeth

"WELL! WHERE ARE WE off to first? Bond Street?" Mr. Bingley still clasped Jane's hand around his elbow, though both were pink in the cheeks and too bashful to look up at each other in the carriage. Their insistence on sitting beside one another left my burglar and me on the other seat—although *we* were not touching constantly and staring into each other's eyes like besotted fools.

"Exeter Exchange," William announced. "I thought the ladies might enjoy the shopping nearby, and then we may admire the animals in the menagerie."

Jane's eyes brightened. "Oh, wonderful! I have not seen that in years."

"Yes, capital," Mr. Bingley agreed. "And once we have amused ourselves, shall we return to my townhouse for tea? Louisa and Caroline—my sisters, Miss Bennet—ought to be returned from their shopping excursion by then. I would be pleased to introduce you."

"Then we are agreed. I am afraid Miss Elizabeth and I will need to step away to attend a bit of business for a few moments. You won't mind, will you, Bingley?"

"Mind? Oh, no! Does that trouble you at all, Miss Bennet?"

Jane was lost in Mr. Bingley's eyes, and she just shook her head.

I leaned over and whispered. "Where are we going? I trust we are not going to The Strand just to admire some lions and tigers."

"Patience, Miss Elizabeth. All will reveal itself in due time."

I scowled at him. "I really wonder why I trust you. I cannot think of one straight answer you have ever given me."

"A sad truth that I hope to amend rather soon," he murmured in my ear. The timbre of his voice and the tickle of his breath were enough to send shivers and prickles racing down my neck and over my scalp. "But let us not burden our companions with such concerns, eh?"

I drew a shaky breath and arranged my skirts over my thighs. It was so much better when I wasn't looking at him, the rascal. He really was too handsome for my own good. "I hope you know what you are about, sir."

"Trust me, Miss Elizabeth. I have as much at stake in this as you do."

"Somehow, I doubt that."

"IS THAT NOT CHARMING? Look, Lizzy. Mr. Bingley showed me this and said he thought it would flatter my face. What do you think?" Jane tilted her head before a mirror, studying the lines of the bonnet Mr. Bingley had offered to buy her.

"It looks beautiful on you, but I think Mr. Bingley would say any-thing flattered your face, and he would be right."

"Oh, Lizzy, you do go on. What do you think of him? Oh, I am *so* glad he is to be our neighbor! I look forward to knowing him better."

"From what I can see," I said, eyeing that gentleman with a smug grin, "no one else in Hertfordshire will get a chance to know Mr. Bingley at all by the time he settles. He is boots over top hat for you already."

Jane giggled behind her hand. "Your associate there is rather clever to have brought him with us. What is his plan?"

I glanced at my "gentleman," who had just returned from another building up the street. He entered the millinery shop where the rest of us had been, and his eyes met mine. And he gave me a single, curt nod.

"I think I'm about to find out. Don't worry about me if I slip out, will you?"

Jane swallowed. "Be careful, Lizzy. I know you want to save Papa and our family's reputation, but your safety is more important. Are you certain you can trust this man?"

My gaze had never left him. Tall, proud, quiet. An enigma I had yet to unravel. But I felt certain of one thing. "Yes, Jane. I will be quite safe with him. I cannot say how I know, but of that, I am sure."

"Then godspeed, Lizzy."

Darcy

"I HAVE MADE ARRANGEMENTS for us to speak with a Mr. Chantrey at the Royal Academy. Now, do stop crossing your eyes at me, Miss Bennet. You will have to look the part of the confident young lady, and the more you look askance at me, the less credible you are."

Elizabeth's feet were still dragging, and she glanced back at the milliner's shop where we had left her sister and Bingley. "But you still have not said a thing about *why*. What are we doing at the Royal Academy? Is that where the sculpture is? Who is this Mr. Chantrey, and what are we to say to him when we meet him?"

"I should say that is a question best left unanswered while we are walking on a public street, Miss Bennet. As for who is Mr. Chantrey, he is one of the brightest young sculptors to have his work chosen for display at the Academy. Why, this year alone, he displayed six busts of prominent figures during the Exhibition, and he has garnered a tremendous reputation already."

"But what has that to do with us?" Her toes were still scuffing along the pavement.

I captured her arm and tucked it more snugly beneath mine. "Why, you see, he will be one of the gentlemen whose opinion is asked for when this 'powerful personage' wishes to have your marble examined."

"Oh, then we ought to be avoiding him, not seeking him out!"

"Not so. As it happens, he employs several assistants in his art and... ah, here we are. Somerset House. What do you think of the archways over the entrance? Very Classical, are they not? And the facade, with the columns—quite tasteful, I think."

She barely glanced up, then fixed her eyes back on me. "Go on. You say this Mr. Chantrey employs assistants? So we must bribe one of them!"

"Miss Bennet, that would be dishonest! What do you take me for? Come now, step lively. He did not mean to remain long at the Academy today, but he agreed to stay to meet with us."

My encouragement had rather the opposite effect, for Elizabeth stopped cold, yanked her hand from mine, and refused to budge. "Not until you tell me what we are doing. Are we going to get the statue back, or are we not?"

"In due time."

One of her slim eyebrows lifted. "I am growing weary of that phrase."

"Look, Miss Bennet, I cannot simply waltz in without finding out if what we seek is even here. Do you think I can read minds? See through walls? Lamentably, I cannot, so if you want me to help you, I need you to cooperate a little. Set aside that massive stubborn streak of yours for the next hour, and see if you cannot act biddable for a change."

She crossed her arms. "I have never acted 'biddable' in my life, and there is no point in trying to pretend now."

I sighed and went back for her, catching her hand again and tugging it free of her little sulk. "And I daresay there is nothing so enticing to any man as a woman with a pertinacious bent, but for a little while, at least behave as if my idea was yours."

"And just what is your idea?"

"Why, Chantrey is looking for assistants to model clay sculptures. That is how he works, you see—setting a draft in clay, as it were, then creating the final masterpiece in marble. He was most pleased when I sent him word that a certain earl of his acquaintance—a patron of his art, naturally—recommended a young lady of good family with a remarkable skill in clay."

Her eyes narrowed. Then, they widened until I could see the full ring of her chocolate irises set against startling white. *"What?* But I don't know how—"

"Ah! And there is one of his assistants now, come to take us in and introduce us." I gestured in greeting to the young man who appeared through a doorway. Elizabeth was still sputtering and gawking, but she allowed me to draw her to my side and present her.

"Mr. Allan Cunningham, may I present Miss Elizabeth Trenton. Miss Trenton descends from a long line of artists in clay, and she has an unparalleled gift for capturing expression and character."

Mr. Cunningham bowed from the waist. "A pleasure, Miss Trenton. Mr. Chantrey is currently attending a modeling session in the Life Academy, but in deference to Miss Trenton's sex, he has agreed to meet with her upstairs in the Antique Academy. If you will follow me, please."

I inclined my head. "Thank you, Cunningham."

Elizabeth let me take her arm, but those dark eyes of hers had blackened and fixed on my cheek. I would not give her the satisfaction of a look until I had shortened our steps enough to fall slightly behind our guide. At last, I risked a glance.

"*Trenton?*" she hissed.

I smiled. "Yes, bit of genius on my part. Your great-great-grandfather's name. So, you see, it is not *entirely* an untruth. Wrong century is all."

"How would you know my great-great-grandfather's name? And what about the rest of that stuff you made up?"

I gave her an innocent look. "If you will think on it for a moment, perhaps you will reflect that I made none of it up. I have never seen a face as expressive as yours. I never actually *told* Cunningham the expressions you captured were in clay."

"What else have you led the man to believe about me? And what is that bit about 'in deference to my sex?'"

I could not help chuckling. "Women are not permitted in the Life Academy," I whispered. "They employ nude models."

"Wait." She held up her finger, and her steps faltered. "Do you mean there is a naked man standing in there while others paint... *all* of him?"

"More likely, it is a female model."

"What?"

"Have I mentioned how convenient it is that you are a woman? Otherwise, Chantrey would probably wish to interview you downstairs. But this works out perfectly for us because I hoped to begin my search in the Antiques Academy, anyway."

"You are not just teasing me again. There is really a live woman back there, and... and..."

"Shh," I hushed her before she could protest again. Cunningham had slowed to wait for us. "You do not want him to see you looking startled by artistic sensibilities. You will give yourself away."

Elizabeth narrowed her eyes. "I am fantasizing about the number of ways I would like to injure you at this moment."

"And I am looking forward to it as much as you are, but I am afraid I must defer the pleasure. Perhaps you will enlighten me later?"

She flashed me one last glare, then fell silent as we spiraled up the magnificent staircase. Cunningham led us from the stairwell into a sumptuously decorated library that served as an anteroom. He asked us to wait a moment as he opened one of the two doors connecting to rooms beyond.

We heard him speaking to someone, then he returned and beckoned us into an apartment that looked purpose built for the instruction of future artists. It was nearly bursting at the seams with castings and busts, all manner of antique artifacts brought there for study. A work table graced the center, with the famous bust of Horne Tooke in the middle. And bent over that was the slightly balding figure of its creator, Francis Chantrey. He looked up as we entered.

"Ah, Miss Trenton. I understand you have applied to join us as an assistant. I regret the Academy does not accept the applications of female students at present, but if your talents meet with my expectations, I may still consider bringing you on. You come with excellent commendations. Now let me hear of you. Where did you learn your craft?"

Elizabeth blinked, and her lower lip trembled. Then her gaze slid to me, just for an instant. She meant to make me pay for this. But if she could get through the next few minutes, I would happily render whatever price she demanded.

Elizabeth

"DO YOU MEAN TO tell me what this was all about? Why did you tell him I was a sculptor? And why did you walk away, leaving me alone with him for ten minutes?"

William smiled and tipped his hat to someone we passed, never averting his eyes from the street. "We needed a way into the building, and it is not the season for public displays. You do not think they just let the doors swing wide for anyone, do you?"

"But what am I to do now? He expects me to return tomorrow, ready to start on sample work for him!"

"I should think it was quite obvious. We return tomorrow, when you will roll up your sleeves and muck about with some clay."

I caught his elbow, none too gently. "I don't know the first thing about clay!"

"I doubt that very much."

A shiver went down my spine, and I lifted my eyes to his. Exactly how much did he know? Had he somehow discovered Papa's little secret? My mouth was moving, but I made only vague gasps.

He glanced at me, raised a brow, then looked beyond me to the building we were approaching. "Ah, here we are—Exeter Exchange. Do you suppose Miss Bennet and Bingley are already upstairs viewing the animals?" He turned us toward the building. Obviously, not intending to answer yet.

I sucked in my breath and bit down on my tongue. *One... Two... Three...*

Oh, it was no good. I couldn't go upstairs and smile at Jane like all would be well when I hardly knew which way I was pointed from one moment to the next. This was positively the most bewildering man I had ever met! I yanked him back. "Will you tell me *what* you are planning?"

"Indeed. But not here. Come, Miss Bennet. I hear they have a new tiger."

"Tiger," I grumbled, falling into step beside him. "I'll show you a tiger..."

"Of that, I have no doubt." He paid out four shillings to the man at the door, granting us access to all three rooms of the menagerie. "Come, Miss Bennet. Have you seen the elephant yet?"

I studied him doubtfully, but he offered his arm, and the way he looked at me... it was as if I could breathe again. Without even saying a word, he seemed to be reassuring me. I had no rational cause in the world to trust him, but sometimes the heart knows what the mind does not.

Apart from that, he had the most irresistible dimples when he smiled.

I closed my eyes, laughing to myself. Someday, I would probably regret all this. But for now, the only thing I felt sure of was that this burglar was the safest person in the world for me to trust.

I gave him my arm, and we climbed the stairs to the first room. At one end towered an elephant, just as William had said. And there were Jane and Mr. Bingley, letting the elephant reach through the bars and take Mr. Bingley's hat off his head with its enormous trunk. Jane offered her handkerchief, and the elephant replaced Mr. Bingley's hat to take the bit of white lace from her hand and dab his face with it. They were both laughing so hard they failed to notice us.

"Come," William said, tugging me by the hand. "The upper floor is better."

"But we have not seen the big cats. What about the tiger? You said the elephant—"

He sighed. "Miss Bennet, I despise being ambiguous, but will you trust me for half a moment? It would delight me beyond measure."

I looked at him—that cryptic smile, the richly rebellious curls of his hair peeking from under his hat, the eyes that seemed to beg me to lean in and drink from those dark pools. My skin flushed, and my pulse quickened. Slowly, I nodded. And I followed him.

This time, as we climbed the stairs, his hand fell to rest at my waist as if he were supporting me. And it was... rather nice. He took no liberties, but his touch was sure, gentle, and comforting. It almost felt like I imagined love might feel—caring, protective. Maybe even affectionate.

My imagination tends to run away with me.

William glanced to the right, where a group was gathered in the room housing the ostrich and the cassowary and other birds. He guided me to the left, toward the quadrupeds. "I have always fancied the hyena. Oh, my! Look at that striped horse. Should you like to ride that, Miss Bennet?"

"I do not ride horses at all," I answered primly. "Papa never taught me."

He looked down at me with a challenging smile. "A sad omission. Someone ought to remedy that. May I ask, what *did* your father teach you?"

"Nothing that will be of any use, I'm afraid."

"No? And I dearly hoped otherwise. My word, look at this strange being. Is it feline or canine?"

We stopped before the hyena's enclosure, and the creature set up such a strange noise that it made the hair on the back of my neck prickle. I jumped... almost into William's arms. "What a hideous sound!"

"Be easy," he murmured close to my ear, making me shiver all over again. "The animal's noise is precisely what I was hoping for."

I rolled my eyes over my shoulder at the odd-looking creature, walking around with its jaws open and emitting the most blood-chilling laughter I had ever heard. "Speak for yourself."

"Yes, it is high time for that, is it not?" He drew out his pocket watch and then replaced it after a brief inspection. "While you were speaking with Chantrey—and not precisely alone, if you recall, for his assistant was present—I asked to be shown to a retiring room for a moment. On my way back to find you, I took the liberty of a brief tour of the building."

I blinked. "And?"

"And I found a young student who had more knowledge than common sense. He was pleased to show me some of the more notable exhibits currently warehoused in an apartment behind the house-keeper's chambers."

"Ah," I breathed. "Did you find anything... ah... interesting?"

"Indeed, I did. About fifty crates, with the contents all boxed up for transport back to the artists who had crafted them and invisible to the eye."

I sagged. "So it could be anywhere?"

"It could be. But my young friend was proud to point out one new arrival that was due to be unpacked and inspected by..." His head lifted, and I realized only then how close we were standing. "Miss Bennet, have you ever beheld an ostrich up close?"

My gaze followed his. We were no longer alone with the quadrupeds, as the people from the next room had come in after us. He captured my hand and placed it on his elbow himself, tipping his hat to the man at the door who was there to check our admission. A moment later, we were camped before a noisy cage of curious birds.

"You were saying?" I asked.

"I will cut to the heart of it. Yes, I believe I have found your sculp-ture, and it is still not unpacked. You are in luck, for the, er, 'person' who purchased it left precise instructions that no one should open the crate until he returns."

"And when will that be?"

"It could be as soon as tomorrow, but I have reason to think it will be at least another day. Miss Elizabeth, I believe we can do this."

I wetted my lips, nodding eagerly. "Yes? What, precisely, are we going to do?"

SEVENTEEN

Darcy

I WAS MAD.

Or lost.

Perhaps a little of both. But when Elizabeth Bennet looked at me that way, with the little wrinkle of amusement at the edge of her mouth, the light catching her eyes, and her lips so softly parted in anticipation, I think I would have leaped into that lion's den for her.

What I proposed, though, was insanity. No one in their right mind would attempt it.

"Let us go now!" she cried. "Why take the chance of waiting until tomorrow?"

Trust her not to cower in fear.

"Because," I answered in my most reasonable voice, "I am waiting on someone else. All in—"

"Good time, yes, I know." She sighed, her shoulders drawing up in resolve. "And what do I do while you are fussing with the sculpture?"

"Why, I thought we covered that. You are an aspiring artist seeking employment with one of the most admired sculptors of our time."

"But he told me himself that he has never employed a female and was not terribly inclined to do so now. It was only on the strength of some Earl of Matlock's commendation that he even planned to grant me a trial, but I do not know any such earl!"

I smiled. "I know you do not."

Her mouth tugged to the side. "I suppose you do. What, did you try to steal all the portrait miniatures from his gallery?"

"My relationship is somewhat more amiable than that."

She crossed her arms. And heaven help me, but it was all I could do not to let my gaze drop to the rather glorious enhancement that posture made of her already fascinating figure. "You really are a mystery to me, sir. You act like the most fastidious and honorable man alive, yet I have caught you in the very act of stealing."

I shrugged. When this was all over, I was going to tell her everything. I'd take her to Darcy House and Pemberley and see if my houses suited her. "You must trust your own eyes, of course."

"I am beginning to doubt everything they tell me where you are concerned." She shook her head and waved her hands as if wiping clean her thoughts. "But that is neither here nor there. What I want to know is how you expect me to get through this sculpture trial long enough for you to do... whatever it is you need to do."

"Well, now, that ought to be simple enough. Chantrey himself will not even be there."

"But a dozen others will. They are students working under a master, and I am to join in their company and work from the same drawings to produce a bust. And then there are guards about, keeping watch on all that valuable art in storage, and did I forget to mention that *I do not know what I'm doing?*"

An ostrich reached through the bars just then, his head hanging just above Miss Elizabeth's shoulder, and made a screeching sound beside her ear. She flinched and instinctively reached for my hand before she turned to look at that offensive bird. I laced my fingers through hers, stroking the inner part of her palm with my thumb. I couldn't help it. She was positively delectable—piquant and sassy, but sweet and strong and sensible all at the same time.

I was mad. Or lost.

Far from withdrawing her hand from mine, Elizabeth tightened her fingers. She had even rested her other hand on my forearm as she edged away from that curious ostrich. The giant bird had taken a liking to her bonnet, pecking and tugging at it as she pulled away. Instead of being outraged or fearful, Elizabeth laughed. "He really is magnificent, is he not?"

I gazed down at her. "Yes. Magnificent."

"Come!" She tugged my hand toward the vultures' cage. "I have questions for you, and fond as I am of that ostrich, I do not think I can manage a straight face with him poking at the feathers on my bonnet. Now, then. How am I to play this part tomorrow?"

"Oh, I should think it would not be so very difficult. You will scarcely make a beginning before I am ready to slip out, and then you will feign illness. In a room full of males, not one of them will doubt or question you."

"Not on the illness part, anyway. But the rest..."

I smiled and leaned down to her ear. "Come, Miss Elizabeth. You must know at least a little about how to mold clay. I cannot believe you have never seen it done before."

She stiffened and regarded me suspiciously. "And where do you think I have seen this?"

"Oh, I am sure I do not know. But you live in the country, do you not? Surely, it is not so unheard of that some villager of your acquaintance might make clay pots. For flowers or something."

Her throat bobbed, and she sucked her lower lip between her teeth. "Do you know, William, being around you is frightfully nerve-wracking."

I chuckled. "If you will allow me? That ostrich loosed one of your hairpins."

Elizabeth froze, only her eyes following my hand as I caught the wayward curl plucked from the back of her head. Her hair was soft as satin and glossy as jet, and it spiraled around my finger. I knew not the first thing about fixing a woman's hair, but it was a diverting study. A twist here, a gentle tuck there, and her hair looked... I gulped.

Lost. That was what I was.

Elizabeth's breath was nearly as ragged as mine. Perhaps that was the first time a man had touched her hair. She carefully felt my handiwork, her eyes still on my face and her chin lifting. "Thank you," she whispered, the puff of her breath warm against my skin.

I had to close my eyes and swallow. Another half a moment, and I would make a public spectacle of us, taking her in my arms and kissing her the way she'd kissed me in the woods.

I coughed. "Of course. Come, Miss Elizabeth. Perhaps we ought to rejoin Bingley and your sister."

Elizabeth

I NEEDED AIR, OR I was going to swoon right there on the floor. It was only a mercy that Jane and Mr. Bingley were so lost in each other's presence that they hardly seemed to notice.

It was time for us to depart anyway, and Jane accompanied me to a little shop to admire some ribbon while the gentlemen secured the carriage. She could not cease the giddy smiles or fits of nervous giggles whenever I looked at her. She was losing face even now as we admired a length of blue satin.

"Mr. Bingley loves blue," she said. And giggled.

"I should think he would. It is my favorite shade on you, as it brings out your eyes."

"Oh, Lizzy! Do not tease me." She bit her lip, playing with the ribbon, then looked up. "Do you really think he likes me?"

Oh, good grief. "Jane, I think if he liked you more, we would have to call a doctor to revive him. The man was smitten with you from the first glance!"

She sighed dreamily. "He is so very amiable. Handsome, too. And I like how easy he is—what I mean is that he was ready to laugh and enjoy himself at every turn, even when the lion kept roaring whenever he tried to talk. He only laughed and tried again because he is so modest. Not stodgy like..." She stopped herself and lifted a shoulder. "Like some men."

"Do you mean like the other gentleman?"

Jane lifted one shoulder. "He seems a little more difficult to know."

"That is putting it mildly. But whatever he is, he is not stodgy."

"Well, I guess you would know. So? Does he have... you know... any ideas? Will you be able to do what you hoped?"

I held my breath and nodded carefully. "I think so. But tomorrow. We have to return tomorrow."

"Tomorrow?" Jane's brow furrowed. "But what will we tell Aunt Gardiner?"

"I suppose we tell her that your Mr. Bingley asked to take you out driving. The weather is still fair, and Hyde Park is beautiful."

A slow smile warmed my sister's face, and then she dipped her head and laughed. "I would not want to impose on his time."

"Believe me, Jane. He won't see it as an imposition." I put the ribbon back on the shelf, and we casually wandered around the corner toward a display of lace. Two more ladies had just entered the shop, and they stood across from us, looking over the ribbons we had just left.

"I tell you, I have never seen the like," one of them said. "The man was so besotted he never even noticed me!"

"No! I do not believe it," her friend replied.

"Upon my word, it is so," the first lady assured her. "He was holding her hand! Not merely escorting her by letting her take his arm. I declare he would not turn loose her fingers and never looked at anything else."

"Come, Jane," I whispered, tugging at my sister's sleeve. "Let us not eavesdrop on their pleasant little gossip session."

"Hmm?" Jane had not even noticed. Naturally. She was sliding her fingers down a bit of hand-worked lace, pinned to a shelf as a sample of what could be ordered. "What are you talking about, Lizzy?"

"Come on. Let's give them their space." I inclined my head toward the ladies on the other side. I could not see more than the tips of their bonnets, but I could still hear their whispers. They weren't trying to be quiet.

"Well!" one of them huffed. "That will put out a dozen debutantes this Season! I know for a fact that Lady Susan had her heart set on him."

"Lady Susan never stood a chance. He would wed the Earl of Matlock's daughter, Lady Sarah, long before he would ever look at Lady Susan."

The first woman laughed. "Whatever came of Lady Catherine's daughter, Anne? I heard a rumor years ago that they were arranged."

"Stuff and nonsense. Lady Catherine started that rumor to force his hand, but Fitzwilliam Darcy is far too stubborn to submit to the likes of her."

I wasn't trying to listen. Truly, I was not. But those names... the Earl of Matlock—William had said that name, too. And hearing it again, I remembered—it was the man my father had said arranged the sale of the sculpture for the Prince! And Lady Catherine, Mr. Collins' patroness, who had tried to purchase it first. My skin prickled with recognition. But what made my pulse race and my knees weak was the last name. *Fitzwilliam.*

Darcy.

I blinked and grabbed a shelf to steady myself. Papa had mentioned that name, too. But this was the first time I had heard the surname, and the given name in the same breath.

Fitzwilliam Darcy.

It all made sense now.

"Jane." My voice didn't work right. I swallowed and tried again, more loudly this time. "*Jane!*"

"Hmm?"

"We have to go. *Now.*"

Darcy

"B INGLEY, MAY I SPEAK frankly for a moment?"

We were standing on the kerb, awaiting his carriage, while the ladies wandered inside a nearby shop. He was smiling like a simpleton, his gaze unfocused, and he scarcely attended me. I had to repeat my question before he blinked and shook himself.

"I beg your pardon, Darcy. You were saying?"

"I was saying that there are things you ought to know about Miss Bennet—her family, her situation in life. You seem quite enamored of the lady."

His brow wrinkled. "Well, it was you who introduced me to her. Do you disapprove?"

"Far from it. Miss Bennet appears to be everything that was claimed about her. But you ought to know that an alliance with the Bennet family will bring you few advantages. I would expect she has very little dowry to speak of, and I have some reservations about the manner in which Mr. Bennet conducts his family."

Concern darkened Bingley's cheerful countenance. "Anything specific?"

I sighed and looked out on the street. "Nothing I can share without violating a confidence. And do not think I am attempting to warn you off the lady. I have seen…" How to say it? "There is a rare strength and quality present in Miss Elizabeth that I should think would override almost any objections. Perhaps the same is true of Miss Bennet. I only wished to advise you to proceed with caution before forming any sort of attachment."

"But Darcy, I have never known anyone like Miss Bennet! What care have I for fortune or politics? I have quite enough money to suit me, and my sisters are well-looked-after." He frowned. "I suppose there is still Caroline to marry off. You would not, by any chance, have a taste for redheads?"

"Sorry to disappoint, but I have discovered a fascination for brunettes."

"Ah, well. I know Caroline would like me to choose a wife who could bring her into higher circles, but I should rather select a lady who delights my eyes and my soul. So, while I appreciate your words of caution and shall take them into consideration, I would not turn from Miss Bennet lightly. I fancy I have met the lady I shall marry."

I smiled. Then laughed. "Bingley, I like you."

He looked bewildered. "I rather hoped you did. This is not some condescending way of telling me I am simple and guileless, is it? I know I am, and it is not necessarily fashionable—"

"No, nothing of that kind. I have few enough friends who count character above circumstances. It is refreshing."

"Is that a compliment, Darcy?"

"Of the highest order. Ah, here is the carriage. And look, the ladies are coming out to rejoin us at precisely the right moment."

Bingley and Miss Bennet locked gazes, and there was no talking to either of them after that. It promised to be a quiet carriage ride, with the two of them simply staring into each other's eyes. I chuckled and went to Elizabeth to offer my arm.

But she did not take it.

As Bingley helped Miss Bennet into the carriage, Elizabeth held back, her shoulders high and her eyes flashing.

"Miss Elizabeth? Is something amiss?" I asked.

She swallowed. "I have questions. Mr. Darcy."

Eighteen

Elizabeth

H E DIDN'T FLINCH. NOT even an eyelash flickered. But his smile cooled, and his chest lifted in a thoughtful sigh. "I imagine you do. Perhaps we might discuss your questions somewhere more... advantageous than a public walk. If you are amenable?"

That was as good as a confession of sorts. I stared at him for a few more seconds, but Jane was already in the carriage with Mr. Bingley, and there was little else I could do. I walked past Mr. Darcy and got into the carriage with the footman's help. He followed a vast deal more slowly, and settled on the opposite end of the cushion. His eyes never left me, but I was determined to ignore him, so I turned toward the window.

"Miss Bennet, do you fancy a turn in Hyde Park tomorrow?" Mr. Bingley asked.

I looked over at my sister. Had Mr. Darcy suggested that? How could he have echoed my very words? It had seemed a pleasant solution to the problem of leaving the house tomorrow without arousing my aunt's concern, but now, I was not so sure. I had just unmasked my "burglar," and it sounded like he was not at all the person I thought he was when we first met.

But Jane knew nothing of my reservations, and she accepted immediately. So, that was that. Jane, at least, would be going on a romantic outing tomorrow. And I would take my chances with Mr. Darcy. I glanced his way—quite accidentally, I assure you—and found his unblinking gaze still fixed on me.

The longer I sat beside him, the more questions I had.

WE DISEMBARKED AT MR. Bingley's townhouse, as he had promised Jane a tour and an afternoon tea with his sisters. She was looking forward to meeting them, but when we discovered they had not yet returned from their own shopping trip, I caught Mr. Darcy's audible sigh of relief.

He shook his head when I sent him a swift look. "I see your question already, Miss Elizabeth. I can only offer the excuse that we had much business to discuss. Bingley," he said, turning to our host, "do you suppose Miss Elizabeth and I might borrow your library for a moment?"

"Yes, yes, of course. I have only a small assortment compared to the vast collection you must have at Pemberley, but you are perfectly welcome to them."

Mr. Darcy stiffened. "Ahem. Yes, thank you, Bingley."

I doubt Mr. Bingley noticed how he made his friend flinch at the name of his estate. The name meant nothing to me, but it was one more confirmation of the thing I had begun to suspect. I was not in league with a high-society art thief, after all, but a man with the power and wealth to bury my poor, reckless father. And that terrified me.

His look told me, if nothing else might have, that all pretense was now at an end. There was a gravity in his features, a hesitation in his posture when he gestured toward the hall. "Will you join me, Miss Elizabeth?"

I squared my shoulders, lifted my chin, and walked before him down the hall and into Mr. Bingley's library. Mr. Darcy closed the door behind us.

"I do not ask where you heard my name, for it matters not. Perhaps I was wrong to keep that detail from you, and I had been seeking a time and place to tell you everything. I pray you understand that my intentions, at least, were benevolent." He looked away, fidgeting with his fingers. "However poor I was in my execution."

"Let us start with Netherfield. Why would you not simply tell me who you were back then?"

He studied me and nodded slowly. "Very well. I suppose the truth is less fantastic than the fabrication. Bingley had questions about those lovely vases over the mantel—questions he needed answered before he finished signing the lease. And, I have some experience in these matters, so he asked me to have a look. The housekeeper was away, so we got in the best we could—through the window."

"That would not be when Mr. Bingley earned his black eye, would it?"

Mr. Darcy's sober features lightened somewhat. "You have an excellent memory, Miss Elizabeth. His nose was bleeding rather profusely, so I escorted him outside and returned to look at the vases. Curious specimens."

My face heated. He had gone there purposely to view my father's vases? How much did he know? I swallowed, and my eyes dropped as I asked softly, "And what did you find?"

"A Venus."

I blinked. "I beg your pardon?"

"I did not set out to deceive you, Miss Elizabeth. In fact, I never meant for you to know of my presence, but that could not be helped. You took me for a fellow who had been pillaging the local houses and causing all the ladies to swoon in their slippers, and I reasoned it would be almost safer to let you make that assumption than to tell you the inconvenient truth."

"Which is?"

"That I wanted to kiss you from the moment you first threatened to hit me over the head."

"You are not very funny, sir."

"I never claimed to be."

I narrowed my eyes and crossed my arms. "So you were never the Meryton thief?"

He rounded a chair and eased a little closer to me. "Of course not. I am not trying to boast, Miss Elizabeth, but I have never had a material need or desire that I could not afford to satisfy through honest means. However, if it is some help, I discovered—quite by accident—who this amorous thief was. You may be assured that after this, he will not be troubling the good ladies of Meryton any longer."

I swallowed and pinched the bridge of my nose. Well, there went some of my questions, at least. But it reared other, more dangerous questions. "So why were those vases so important?"

Mr. Darcy sighed. "You do go on about those."

"Because I must know! What made you and Mr. Bingley want to look at them, and why—*why* pass yourself off as a thief?"

"Let us forget the vases for now," he growled. "And let me address the more important matter. You are a lady of good reputation, and I enjoy a rather honorable standing in society myself. Which would be easier for you to tell your family: that you had encountered the burglar everyone was talking about and came away with a fine story to tell, or that you had met Fitzwilliam Darcy of Pemberley, Derbyshire, skulking about the neighboring property and inspecting those vases?"

I wetted my lips. "If..." I coughed slightly. "If my mother knew your name... I suspect I would hear no peace on the matter. But why not simply tell me the truth and let me make up my own mind?"

He shook his head. "Pure and simply? I panicked. And that is a deal for me to say, for to anyone who knows me, I am the least flighty, the most stable and reliable gentleman they can name." He took a breath, then drew a cautious step closer to me. "You startled me, Miss Elizabeth, not least because I admired you from the first second and knew not what to do with that feeling."

My heart gave a curious thump. What girl doesn't like to hear a handsome man say he admires her? But I could have endured the confession with perfect equanimity if the gentleman were... oh, I don't know, Mr. Collins. I don't even think Mr. Bingley, sweet as he seemed to be, would have the power to unsettle me. But Mr. Darcy did.

And he knew it.

He came another step nearer and turned his palm up, asking for my hand.

Well, I was already in this over my head, with no way back to shore that I could see. Why not drown a little? I raised my hand, made a nervous fist, then let go of my breath and rested my fingertips on his. I would see what more he had to say.

But it was not his words that convinced me. It was the joy that sparkled in his face just then—his dimples dancing, his smile dashing and delicious. "Miss Elizabeth, thank you for trusting me."

"I did not say I trusted you," I said tartly.

He laughed. "Thank you for giving me an opportunity not to have my head split open again."

"The afternoon is still young."

"Indeed, it is. Very well, then. You are wondering why I keep mentioning those vases from Netherfield."

I gulped. Here it was—the moment I had been dreading for at least fifteen years. Papa was about to be revealed to the world, and life, as our family had enjoyed it, was coming to an abrupt end. "If you are what you say you are, you must already know about them. So, is it that? You are on a quest to bring my father to ruin? You came to see the vases and buy the statue and uncover everything? If that is your intent, I—I..."

He scoffed, still clasping my hand. "Hardly. I could not care less about his vases, but they turned me on to a suspicion. That was why I came back that day to ask you about that sculpture. I did a little research into the archives. Tell me, what do you know about your great-grandfather, Robert Trenton, Viscount Elroy III?"

I narrowed my eyes. "He was no viscount."

"In fact, he was, but his reputation was ruined and his fortune all but erased by the time of his death. Would you like to know how?"

"I have a feeling you're going to tell me."

He shrugged. "Naturally. He was found out as a copyist. That is one thing the Academy expressly forbids in its summer exhibits, and he had misled them. They drummed him out of the Academy after that."

"What?" I frowned. "Are you saying that *he* was the artist who made that sculpture?"

"That I do not know. He was also recognized for his authentic collection, the art he imported from Italy. He was a great admirer of Michelangelo, for example. At nearly the same time as his dismissal from the Academy, his investments turned bad. I understand he sold off whatever he could to pay back his debts, so there must be some reason that this one was kept."

I sniffed. "Perhaps it was his wedding gift to his daughter. I always heard Papa's mother came to her marriage as nearly a pauper. If that was all her father could give her—"

"Or His Royal Highness just bought a worthless rock."

I set my teeth. "And you are involved in the transaction."

He nodded gravely. "At the behest of my uncle, the Earl of Matlock."

My mouth fell open. "Ah," I breathed. "Does he know... any of this?"

Mr. Darcy shook his head. "You may distrust my reluctance to drag my family name into this, and you would be right to do so. I let you be deceived, and it was unforgivable, but pray believe me now when I say that I have as much to lose in this as you do, Miss Elizabeth."

I regarded him for a moment. "Do you know, Mr. Darcy, every feeling of reason or good sense demands I walk away this instant. Wash my hands of you and let my father's indiscretion catch up to him, and the consequences be what they may."

His mouth curved. "But?"

I narrowed my eyes and shook my head at him. "But you do, after all, have a rather nice smile."

"Do I? I expected you to say something noble about coming too far to turn back or saving your sisters from ruin or some such."

"That much goes without saying." I moved closer to him and tipped my face until I was looking at the underside of his chin while he froze in place, scarcely breathing as I patted his chest. "But you seem to be at your most brilliant and most shockingly audacious when I tease you. I believe I will keep using it to my advantage."

I walked to the door and then looked over my shoulder when I reached it. He had his hand over his heart like he was trying to catch his breath, and his eyes were full of bewilderment. "Is that a promise or a threat, Miss Elizabeth?"

I turned the latch and pulled the door open. "I suppose we will find out tomorrow."

Nineteen

Elizabeth

M r. Bingley and Mr. Darcy arrived at eleven the next morning. Aunt and Uncle Gardiner were eager to meet Mr. Darcy,
though more than a little in awe of him as he bowed cordially. The look
on my aunt's face when she first heard his name, I shall never forget.
This Mr. Darcy must be even more wealthy than I had realized.

Which made it even funnier to me that I had first met him cowering
behind a fireplace screen.

"Where are you off to, Bingley?" Mr. Darcy asked casually as we set
out. "The weather today does not favor a turn in Hyde Park."

"Bond Street, I should think," Mr. Bingley replied, his eyes
sparkling at Jane. "Does that suit, Miss Bennet? Wait, Darcy, will you
not be joining us?"

"I am afraid not. Miss Elizabeth and I have business at the Academy,
which should, I hope, be resolved today." His eyes rested on me, his
expression significant.

"Oh. Well, how long shall your business last?"

Mr. Darcy looked thoughtful, his gaze never leaving me. "An hour, I should think. But do not be concerned about us. I have left orders for my coachman to meet us on the Strand. There is no need for you to return for us."

Mr. Bingley shrugged. "Very well, Darcy. A pity you will miss the shopping. I say, when shall we meet again this afternoon?"

"Darcy House. I would be honored to offer the ladies some refreshment after our outing. Miss Elizabeth, will that do?"

I lifted a brow. "I assume it will. Thank you, sir."

He nodded and settled against the squabs, the side of his calf gently bumping into mine. "You are most welcome, Miss Elizabeth. I expect you will need it by the time our errand is complete."

Darcy

B INGLEY'S CARRIAGE SET US down at the Exeter Exchange, and I handed Elizabeth out. Her smile had faded, and she clasped my arm with unusual strength. "Are you certain of this, Mr. Darcy?" she whispered.

I covered her hand with my own. "No. But I am willing to risk a very great deal, so that should reassure you."

She held me in her gaze and nodded. "Let us get on with it, then."

"Not yet. We are waiting for... ah, there he is, across the street already. Come, Miss Elizabeth."

"What are we looking for?" She extended her strides to match mine, which is saying a great deal. I have seldom encountered a woman who can keep up with me when I have a mission on my mind, but Elizabeth Bennet was so readily at my side that I did not realize at first how quickly I was walking. I slowed.

"That man there, standing at the kerb with the hamper," I replied.

"Yes? And who is he?"

I smiled. "My butler."

Elizabeth laughed. "Trust you to bring your butler along when your intention is to burgle something."

"One uses the resources available to him." We reached the corner, and my butler finally saw us. He started to bow, but I stopped him. "That will not be necessary, Dobbs. Thank you. I will take the hamper."

"But, sir, it is rather heavy. Should you not like someone to carry it for you?"

"There is no need. You may take the carriage home and send it back for me."

He bowed again. "Very good, sir."

"Oh, and Dobbs, this is Miss Elizabeth Bennet. She will be joining me for tea this afternoon, along with Mr. Bingley and her sister, Miss Jane Bennet. Will you see to the preparations?"

A curious light appeared in the old man's eyes. Dobbs was too much the professional to smile—a stately smirk was as far as he ever got. But his attention shifted to Elizabeth for an instant. Then he bowed again. "It would be my deepest pleasure, Mr. Darcy."

"What was that?" Elizabeth asked as Dobbs walked back to the mews.

I was busy hefting the hamper and trying to decide how I would carry it. "What was what?"

She leaned her head close to my shoulder, still watching Dobbs's retreating back. "He gave me the strangest smile just there."

"Ah. Well, you see, Miss Elizabeth, you may be the first lady I have voluntarily invited to tea."

She got a quizzical look. "I do not understand."

I settled on carrying the hamper under one arm so I could still offer Elizabeth my other, and I caught her hand. "That is because you do not know Lady Matlock, my aunt. She has made it her mission to find me a wife, but thus far, I have evaded her wiles."

Elizabeth was quiet for several strides as we walked up to the great courtyard. "I still do not understand."

It was my turn to laugh, and I clasped her hand a little tighter. "Then I hope to explain myself better when we have a chance." The door to Somerset House was opened to us, and I escorted her inside. I told our errand to the man at the door, and he asked us to wait while he went for the person we were to see.

"Well now, Elizabeth, are you ready to become a sculptor?" I whispered into her ear.

She shook her head "no" as her mouth puckered. "Y-yes?"

"That's the spirit. Come now, look eager and excited."

"Excited, I can manage. I am not so sure about eager."

I turned to her, and those luminous brown eyes searched mine. She was craving reassurance, and for some spectacularly mysterious reason, she trusted me to give it. So, I did. I set the hamper down and curled my fingers at her cheek, just grazing the nape of her neck.

"It will be well, Elizabeth," I whispered.

She closed her eyes and leaned into my hand. "I wish I could be as sure of that as you are. What if we are discovered? What if—"

"Have I ever told you how beautiful you are, Elizabeth?"

Her eyes widened. She sucked in a breath, and her entire body froze. Slowly, she shook her head.

"Then I will have to tell you later. That will give us both something to look forward to."

Elizabeth chuckled and let her forehead lean against mine. "I am counting on it."

"So am I." I toyed with a curl at her cheek, then let my hand fall and stepped back. "Better now?"

She nodded and let out a long sigh. "Better. By the by, what is in the hamper?"

"This? Oh! You do not mean to work clay dressed like that, do you? I had a frock brought for you."

She tilted her head and studied the hamper. "Is that all? It looks heavier than that."

I smiled and put my finger to my lips. One eyebrow curved, and she nodded in understanding. "I see I will have to wait."

Elizabeth

M R. CUNNINGHAM, WHOM WE'D met yesterday, sent a student named Watson to greet me and show me where I might change. I expected to be shunned as a woman, but Watson was very polite. "I am afraid we have no maid to assist you, Miss Trenton. Can you manage?"

"I have four sisters, and we share a maid—or, rather, I wait until I cannot wait any longer. I am used to making do, thank you very much."

The gentleman bowed courteously, then left me alone. I bolted the door and set my hand on my hips. Time to explore that hamper. I lifted the lid and saw only coarse linen. Curious, I pulled it out and found that it was, indeed, a work gown. But something heavy was wrapped inside it.

I laid it on the floor and peeled back the layers. Inside, I found the answer. And the genius of William's plan.

It was a sculpture of what looked like Athena, about eighteen inches high and set in marble. She held a quiver over her shoulder, and one arm looked as if it had once held a bow, but the hand was broken off.

Where had William got this? It appeared, to my uneducated eyes, at least, to be older than our English hills. No one could doubt its authenticity. The contrast to my father's sculpture could not have been more marked. Surely, this was precisely the sort of thing the prince thought he was buying in the first place.

Was this something William had already owned? Did he take a magical journey to Scotland overnight to buy this from Lord Elgin himself? I would ask him all about it later, but for the first time, I understood what he meant to do. He would replace my father's forgery with the real thing.

And if it worked, we would all be saved.

I EMERGED FROM THE closet that served as a changing room and found William seated in the library anteroom. This was madness. He had the easy job of it, tearing open a crate and switching the sculptures. I was the one who had to carry on a convincing act before strangers. Could I manage it? I thinned my lips in determination and gave him a single nod. I'd do my best.

Then I went to the gentleman who had shown me to the room. "I have left my hamper in the closet, so I might change again later. Will it be safe, or ought I to move it?"

"Perfectly safe, Miss Trenton. You are the only lady here today, so the room will remain undisturbed. I will lock the door for you, however, to be certain that your belongings are not troubled."

"Oh! I am sure there is no need for that," I protested, sending William a swift glance.

"It is a precaution I am happy to offer. I cannot guard the door, and I will not see a lady forced to ride home wearing a gown covered in clay, in case her belongings are disturbed."

"Oh, but surely, no one would—"

"I can retrieve the hamper and keep it with me," William offered.

The man and I both looked over at him. "I would not wish to trouble you, sir," he said.

"It is no trouble. I mean only to recline here with a book while Miss Trenton exhibits her skill. What if she completes her task before you are available to unlock the door to the changing room for her?"

I closed my eyes and murmured a silent prayer. If the man insisted on locking the door, we would have to think of something else. How to convince him without looking suspicious?

He looked thoughtful and then bowed. "Very well. I would not wish to inconvenience a lady."

My sigh of relief was audible. All this tomfoolery was beyond me, and I made a terrible thief. It was a good thing we only had to steal one thing. "Thank you."

"This way, Miss Trenton," the man offered.

I sent William one more half-panicked glance, mouthed "good luck," and followed my guide.

Darcy

T HE FIRST QUESTION WAS how long I should wait.

I could not very well go skulking about, dressed like I lived in Grosvenor Square and carrying a hamper under my arm like a servant without attracting some attention. And Somerset House was not precisely empty. I had counted at least twenty Antiquities students passing through the library to one of the lecture halls. But when the door closed, and I heard the instructor commence speaking, I decided there would be almost no one on the stairs for the next hour, at least. I took up the hamper and proceeded to the staircase with all the stately grace I could muster.

Somerset House was six floors, gutted straight through with that magnificent spiraling staircase. At the uppermost floor was the Grand Hall, where the choicest paintings would line the walls from floor to glass ceiling in the early summer. Visitors counted the breathtaking architecture—the beautiful staircase and the expansive hall—to be part of the experience.

But the place I needed to go was somewhat humbler—down one floor and almost directly under the room Elizabeth occupied right now. These rooms were not open to the public. Rather, they were used by the housekeeper for her residence and storage. And for tools.

Rather convenient.

I glanced around, turning my head slowly so no one might think that I was actually looking for anything. Men of my station were expected merely to survey, not to search for anything in particular. The ceilings on most floors were lavishly adorned with intricate plaster designs, but this floor was painfully sparse by comparison. There was little for me to pretend to admire, in case anyone should think to wonder what I was about.

But fortunately, we had come at a rather quiet time of day. Most of the Academy's students were in class, and the housekeeper ought to be in the kitchens about now. It was child's play to pick the lock—I would probably suffer some moments of disquiet in my conscience later about that.

I was not proud of the things I had learned from George Wickham in my youth, but this once, at least, I found that knowledge useful. Shades of gray had plagued this entire debacle, but one thing I was sure of—Elizabeth was innocent, and whatever cause she championed had to be right. So I would help *her;* not for myself or anyone else. But the beauty was that in helping her, everyone would be served fairly—even if a few laws were technically broken. I just had to carry out my task as quickly as possible, so I didn't have time to doubt myself.

I closed the door and moved swiftly through the rooms until I reached the one where I had discovered the crate. And miracles must be real, because it was still there, undisturbed. A few minutes more, and I found a bar with which to pry the nails from the wood. This part I undertook with patient care, for not only was I keenly interested in remaining quiet, but I also meant to nail the top back on the crate when I was done. I dared not damage it.

It seemed stupidly easy. The nails slipped from the oak almost soundlessly, and when I pawed through the thick nest of straw, I found the sculpture.

It was just as Elizabeth had described to me—Eros seducing Psyche, his wingtips wrought in glorious feathery detail, and the agony and passion in their faces almost flesh-like in their faithfulness. Seconds mattered, but I could not help taking a few of them simply to admire the masterpiece I was stealing from the Prince. Truly, it was evocative and magnificently wrought, no matter its true heritage. I would have delighted in owning it myself.

But I liked my neck still better.

I opened the hamper, thinking only to pull out the Athena marble that George Wickham had managed to pillage from Lady Catherine... but it was carefully swathed in Elizabeth's gown. I hadn't considered that having donned the work dress from the hamper, she would re-wrap the statue in her own... her own...

This... ah, this could take me a moment.

A gentle hint of lavender bathed the gown's presence and sank into my senses. *Angels in heaven.* Surely, Athena did not smell that good. For an instant, no longer, I lifted the lacework of her bodice to my face. Indeed, this was something that would require further investigation. Perhaps later, once she was wearing that gown again. And I could ask her some questions that had nothing to do with art and everything to do with *her* being a masterpiece.

I coughed and got back to business.

It seemed an eternity, but it was probably mere moments before the switch was complete. I tapped the last nail into place and righted the crate exactly where I had found it. Then I eased back, letting my hammering heart drop to a slow thud.

It was done. And if I could retrace my steps up to the next floor without raising anyone's suspicions, all would be well.

I smoothed down the front of my waistcoat, forced a few slower breaths, and straightened, the hamper under my arm. A quick dash through the housekeeper's rooms, and I was back outside, ready to look as if I were bored. Waiting for Elizabeth.

Except... there was Elizabeth now. She was slipping down the stairs faster than her feet could carry her, only keeping upright because she had a death grip on the railing. She was looking around frantically, and when her eyes landed on me, she moved even faster.

"Elizabeth? Was your sculpture work that bad already?"

She waved for silence. "We must not be seen! Can we hide in there?" she whisper-shouted at me.

"In here? This is the last place we should... wait, hide? What do you mean, hide? We can do no better than to stroll casually away as if nothing were amiss."

Her head jerked to the side, and I saw her staring down the center of the spiral stairs. Her hand went to her mouth. That was when I realized the voices outside had grown from the random echo of conversation to shouts and excitement. Elizabeth ran to me and closed the door of the housekeeper's apartments. "We must hide now!"

"What is happening? Do not be silly, I—"

"Oh, will you stop arguing, William? The Prince is here! Now! And he's coming up to the Antiquities Academy!"

TWENTY

Elizabeth

I WAS NOT LYING when I told William—that is, Mr. Darcy—that I didn't know the first thing about crafting clay. I had watched my father for years, but never from start to finish on any one project. And besides, Papa made vases, which I fancy must be very different to busts.

How was I even to make a pretense at this? Should I wet the clay some more? Or pinch it into eye sockets and a rough nose-shape? I could probably manage that. Where would a real sculptor begin?

But Mr. Cunningham received me graciously. It was like he didn't even know I was hyperventilating with panic. He showed me the place I was to work, the tools laid out for me, and then presented me with two sketches of a man's portrait. "These are the drawings Mr. Chantrey would like you to work from. As you see, there is a sketch of the front and profile. Is there anything else you require to make your beginning?"

"Oh, no," I replied airily. "I like to pass a few moments in silent contemplation before I begin. It... ah... centers my thoughts."

He inclined his head slightly. "Very good. Mr. Chantrey will look in on you in half an hour. Will that suit?"

I smiled. They were leaving me alone? Well... alone in a room of about a dozen male students. But I didn't have to carry out this ruse in front of the men who would look at my work? *Perfect.* "Thank you, Mr. Cunningham."

The door closed, and I drank in a long sigh. William would be finished before I could do much damage here. But I should at least look busy, because the males in the room kept glancing at me. Let me see, now... I examined the sketches and held them up before the lump of clay I had been given. This couldn't be that hard. It was the face of some older man, no one I would recognize. Where should I start?

Well, should I pick up that knife-looking tool there and start drawing hair on the thing? A little cut here, a cut there... I stood back to evaluate the effect. Not... conventionally accurate. Certainly not Grecian curls at the forehead like the drawing, but if one closed one eye, and used a little imagination, that sort of looked like hair.

I peeked through the corner of my eye and saw one man sweeping his thumbs over the cheeks of the bust he was creating, smoothing and sculpting it to perfection. Well, I had fingers too. I could push some clay from the sides of the lump forward... there. That was almost oblong now, like cheekbones and a nose. I tilted my head and squinted. A very *big* nose.

That would not do. I squashed it back where it was before—roughly—and tried to re-shape it. But the more I played with it, the less pliable the clay felt. I frowned, then snapped my fingers. Water! Papa used more water when he did not like the feel of his clay.

But not that much.

Oh, dear.

How long does it take for clay to dry back out after it has been saturated into slime? I bit my lip and cringed as I evaluated the mess I'd made. At least the hair looked... smoother. Ahem.

I stuck my tongue out and closed one eye as I worked to slick the ooze off the face of the bust and find the drier clay beneath. The man in the drawing had thin cheeks, anyway. It was a good thing I wore that work gown, because I would have ruined my own by now. As it was, my arms were coated with glop up to my elbows, and I couldn't distinguish one finger from the other any longer.

Oh, and everyone kept looking at me. Perhaps it was because I was the only female, or perhaps it was because there was a clay-tinted puddle dripping on the floor at my feet. But I felt like I was actually making progress. A little practice and I might become a true proficient at this.

That was when the shouting began.

My heart stopped. Had William been discovered? I froze in place, my hands still dripping with sludge and my eyes darting from one door to the next as more men began racing through the room. I couldn't make sense of anything they said until I heard Chantrey himself slamming through the doors and barking orders at people.

"Look sharp, there, lad!" he'd say to one young man. Then, to another, "Run for Cunningham, and take these out! You, there, bring the table in, and all the lanterns you can find!" He was dashing back and forth, then he stopped at me.

Thank goodness he wasn't looking at the bust. I gulped and moved to stand in front of it.

"Miss Trenton, I am afraid I must ask you to take your leave. I am sorry to be discourteous, but His Royal Highness's carriage has just stopped outside the courtyard."

I blinked. "But... but I..."

"I do apologize, but I will be wanted. In five minutes, this room will be crawling with the prince's men, and..." He shook his head. "It is best if you go. Another time, Miss Trenton."

I swallowed, my pulse thundering in my ears. "Y-yes. I... thank you. Where shall I—"

But Chantrey was gone, and I was standing stupidly in the middle of a room that now buzzed with chaos. An instant later, I came to myself. I found a rag to wipe the worst of the clumpy goo off my hands, and then I ran for the stairs. William could be in terrible danger.

Darcy

"**B**ACK HERE," I HISSED. "Elizabeth!"

She was peeking through the door with one eyeball, trying to watch for the very instant the prince's men ascended the stairs. When I tugged at her sleeve, she jumped and spun around, her hand over her heart. "Oh, you scared me!"

"If you find that frightening, I suggest you follow me, or you will know true fear. Come! We should not have cornered ourselves in here."

Elizabeth followed, snagging my elbow like her life depended on it and nearly ripping my shoulder out of its socket. It hurt, but I'd got used to her injuring me. And I didn't mind any longer. "I didn't know where else to go. I couldn't stay where I was."

I stopped and pointed at the door. "Don't you realize that if the prince is here to see that statue, someone will come in here to retrieve it?"

She paled. "Oh, dear. I didn't think—I just wanted to get to you. I thought if... if..."

"Oh, never mind. If we must hide, there could be worse places. Quickly! There are a dozen more crates back here we can duck behind." I grabbed her hand and pulled her deeper into the room. There must be a closet or a stack of wooden boxes or...

"There!" Elizabeth pointed. "Can we fit in that?"

Cold sweat beaded on my brow. She was pointing at a long trunk, probably used for storing linens and dust shrouds. The lid stood open, it was enormous, and it looked almost empty. But we would have to lie down together to fit inside.

Good heavens.

"Surely we can find something more suited to... ah. There, that one in the back. Quickly!" I stowed the hamper with the fake sculpture behind a box in a darkened corner. Then I ushered Elizabeth before me to a large, upright crate that looked to be built for transporting a life-sized sculpture. There was a pallet leaning against it that would form a sort of lid when it was nailed together, and I pulled it after us to hold against the open front like a door.

Elizabeth's breath puffed in quick gasps, and she put her hands to the wood. Cracks of light splintered through from the outside, and there was a knothole just large enough for one person to peer out of. Elizabeth pushed her face to it, jostling against me, so I had to shuffle to the back of our odd little box.

The "floor" of the crate was still mounded with straw, just above my ankles, and with every move we made, it crackled under our feet. We would have to remain absolutely still. I sucked in a ragged breath and tugged at my cravat.

A thousand nerves seemed to rip and fire all at once through my body. Pressed up against Elizabeth's... er, the back of her gown, I would have to be dead not to note the warmth of her thigh leaning on mine through that thin fabric. And it didn't seem to matter what she wore—her curves were impossible to conceal, as was that delirious lavender-water freshness. It must have been coming from the sumptuous chocolate curls trailing at the nape of her neck. I took out my handkerchief and mopped my forehead.

But torment though it was to practically cradle Elizabeth in my arms, it was made ten times worse when we exhausted the fresh air in our little cabinet. Within seconds, my lungs felt ready to collapse, and every breath required heavy effort, pulling just a trickle of cool air through the cracks. I'd never quite got over the terror of Richard locking me in the closet under the stairs when I was nine, and now it was worse.

Now, we were hiding for our lives.

"I think they're trying the key for the outer door," Elizabeth whispered.

I pulled her back. "Best get comfortable, so we do not have to move again once they come in."

She gave me a peculiar look. "But I was comfortable."

I coughed. "Yes, well... that posture is untenable for me. I suggest we shift face-to-face, like so. And now we can take turns looking through the knothole."

Elizabeth shrugged and complied, letting me turn her and maneuver her, so she was not so intimately pressed against me. With opposite corners to back ourselves into, now I stood a chance of escaping without completely losing countenance. But the straw under our feet made a fearful racket with every shift of our weight.

"Shh!" Elizabeth put her hands on my chest, stopping me from moving. "They're coming!"

I gulped a long pull of air—it might be the last I would get for a while—and clasped my hands over hers. And I closed my eyes, trying to pretend I was simply in my own darkened bedroom. With her delicious fingers crawling up my shoulders to my throat, and her sweet hair tickling my nose, and...

Hang that idea.

I'd pretend I was dead. That was probably safer.

"William, what is the matter with you?"

I opened my eyes and realized that I'd been swaying dizzily. Elizabeth grabbed me by the lapels and pushed me upright. "You're going to fall against that slat and give us away!"

My face was clammy, and I shook my head to help me see better. It didn't help. "I don't... this is not such a good idea. We should find someplace better."

"There isn't anyplace better! You're making too much noise, and will you stop gulping like that?"

I swiped the perspiration off my upper lip. "It is simply that I am not good in close spaces. A rather terrifying experience when I was a youth, and I..."

"Oh, good grief. You dragged us in here, and you're claustrophobic?"

My heart was hammering, and I could scarcely draw enough breath to answer her. I just nodded in the darkness.

I heard Elizabeth sigh, but it was not an impatient sound. "Come here," she whispered.

"I can't get much closer. You're standing on my toes already."

"No. *Here*." She cupped my chin, and an instant later, I didn't care if I could breathe. It didn't matter if I suffocated. I would die happy because Elizabeth was brushing her soft mouth against mine. Her hands were curiously rough, but they were all I wanted as she held my face between them, pulled me down, and consumed me. She was generous, too—not just one little butterfly of her lips caressing mine. I felt like a flagon of wine, opened and poured forth and drunk with abandon.

I should be jealous that she was so good at this. She nibbled my lower lip, sucking it between her teeth and then smiling, wide-mouthed against my chin. She was a perfect minx, and I wanted more. I groaned softly, but no longer in fear of confinement. My mind filled with all the things I would do to her if she were mine, and we were at Pemberley as man and wife.

She belonged at Pemberley.

"Elizabeth," I breathed. "Would you—"

"Shut up, you noisy man." She cupped her hands behind my head and kissed me harder. Well... I suppose my question could wait.

My skin was racing with an all-new sort of panicked thrill. This was glory, this was what I was born for. It was like all my life had been building to this one point—five minutes alone with Elizabeth Bennet in a wooden packing crate. Hiding from our own ruin.

"Better now?" she murmured against my ear.

"Ungh..." That was the most intelligent thing I could say. So much for a Cambridge education.

Elizabeth laughed and kissed the divot in the center of my chin. Then her hands slid back to my chest when a key rattled in the lock. We heard the door open, and footsteps followed. My heart dropped with each step. One person. No, two. But that was all. I forced my breathing to dip a little more because it was echoing like thunderclaps in that hollow crate. Heaven only knew how loud we were from the outside.

"Is this the one?" we heard someone ask.

"Yes, that one."

"Do we pry off the top now?"

"No," the second man replied. "His Highness wishes to observe the unpacking. We will carry it as it is."

"Jolly good. You take that side."

I clasped Elizabeth's hands more tightly. They would pick up the bloody crate and carry it off, and then we could leave safely. I started counting the beats of her pulse through her fingertips. It could not be more than ten or twenty seconds more.

"Hold there!" a third voice called.

There was a heavy sound as the two workers put the crate down.

"Leave it. His Highness is impatient and does not wish to wait until it is carried upstairs. He will see it here."

There was a silence, during which I was certain Elizabeth stifled a panicked sob.

"But there be no lanterns here," one man protested. Good man.

"Nevertheless, His Highness does not wish to climb any higher than this floor."

I rolled my eyes. Prinny was afflicted with gout—no doubt because all he did was eat and carouse. I could not say I was surprised that his royal slothfulness extended that far, but if he was that reluctant to climb just one more flight of stairs, why not avoid all of them and simply have the statue carried down to the Life Academy? But there was nothing I could say from where I was.

Elizabeth sucked in a breath of apprehension, stiffening still more. I made a shushing motion with my mouth, emitting no sound but brushing my lips against her hair so she could feel my reassurance. We were safe where we were, so long as no one discovered us.

TWENTY-ONE

Elizabeth

I HAD NEVER HEARD a prince's voice before. I didn't care for it.

"Now, then," the Regent said as all others fell silent. "Let us have it out."

I jumped against William's chest when a dreadful screech filled the room. Men were prying off the top of the crate and carrying it aside. Would all be as he expected to find it? Would our little replacement be discovered?

I bit my lip and turned my face into William's cravat. Well, why not? He didn't seem to mind. And he smelled nice. His hands slipped to my waist, and I leaned into him a little more. I could get used to leaning on him.

We could hear the rustling of the packing straw, some thumping, and then a staggered series of gasps and "Aaahh"s.

"Well, take it out, Chantrey," the Prince ordered. "What is it?"

There was a moment of relative silence. Then we heard Chantrey's voice. "It looks to be a miniature of the statue of Athena, Your Highness."

"But I thought this thing was supposed to be a statue of Cupid. Where is the Cupid sculpture?"

More silence. I pressed my face harder into William's shoulder.

"But this is what was sent, Your Highness," another man said. "I collected it myself from Longbourn, and this is the very crate. I would know it anywhere."

"I recall what was written, and it said a sculpture of Cupid seducing Psyche. I was rather looking forward to seeing that," the Prince complained.

No one said anything for several seconds, but then Chantrey spoke up. "If I may, Your Highness, what you have is far more valuable. This is clearly Athena, the patroness of the great Parthenon. What is Cupid compared to the great goddess?"

I was listening with my heart in my throat when something brushed against my leg. I flinched, then looked accusingly at William. This was no time for that sort of play. But he acted perfectly innocent.

"What?" he whispered.

"You're petting my leg with your foot! Now, of all times?"

"I swear, I did not."

"Then what..." The Something thumped against my calf again, and this time I nearly jumped into his arms. Whatever it was, it was thrashing on the floor, moving the straw heap and skittering in circles. I couldn't help it. I squeaked.

Then I climbed William.

He grunted and let loose an impolite word or two as I clambered up his shoulders, but he caught me. "What the blazes are you doing?"

"Shh... there it is! What *is* that?"

William shifted his weight, trying to keep us both upright without crashing through our makeshift door. But it seemed our scuffling had not gone unnoticed.

"Do you hear that?" the prince asked his men. "I say, there was the strangest squeak just now and some thrashing about."

The prince's question made my soul turn to lead. I buried my face in William's neck and prayed he wouldn't drop me. Fine chance of that—his hands were firmly clasped under my posterior, and he wasn't letting go.

"I heard nothing, Your Highness," someone said.

"But I was sure of it! Have you any vagrants hiding amongst the buckets and brooms here?"

"No, Your Highness, for the doors are kept locked. Perhaps it was the housekeeper," another voice suggested.

"I am quite certain..."

The thumping under my leg had not gone still, and I was terrified to look down. "It is a rat," William whispered. He turned as silently as he could and lowered me behind him. Then, with his toe, he rooted amid the straw until he found the brown creature. "There. You probably stepped on him, poor fellow."

"Poor fellow! He is about to get us hanged!" I shot back. Quietly, of course.

Calmly, William herded the bouncing rodent toward the front of the crate with his foot. The instant the rat saw a crack large enough, it darted away, sending another box toppling over and scratching the floor with its panicked little toes.

"There!" the prince cried. "Someone is back there."

I wrapped my arms around William from behind and banged my forehead on his broad shoulders. Could this get any worse? We were dead. The prince had heard everything, and in a moment, we would be discovered.

Footsteps scattered through the room as men searched among the crates. William turned and wrapped his arms around me. I shivered and clung to him—my burglar, the man who had stolen my heart. At least if we were going to hang for treason, I could say that I knew what the safety of a man's embrace felt like.

I wished I would never have to leave it.

"Look, Your Highness!" someone called. "It was merely a rat trying to escape. Caught by surprise, I shouldn't wonder. He was probably stowed away in this straw."

William and I froze together, and I clamped my fat mouth closed by biting his coat sleeve. If I could keep quiet for just a little longer…

The prince grunted. "Perhaps. Have a rat catcher brought in. Shameful!"

"It will be done, Your Highness," someone promised.

"Now, then, what to do about this Athena statue?"

"Indeed, Your Highness, it is sure to be the jewel of your collection!" one of his men enthused. "Since the issue of the Parthenon Marbles is at stake, Your Highness can do no better than to obtain a decorative sculpture of Athena herself. There can be no doubt of this sculpture's authenticity. It lends credibility to your wish to preserve the collection from Athens."

"How fine this will look on display at Carlton house!" someone else said.

"I think, Your Highness, that the original sender made a mistake. You know, the average country squire probably cannot tell the difference between Athena and Cupid! But the favor is all on your side." This was Chantrey again. "Do you wish to have it examined?"

"Yes, yes. Carry out your study and have it brought to Carlton House," replied the bored voice of the prince. "I will send for Lord Matlock and have the purse sent to Bennet. Where is my Maria? I am famished. Take me to my carriage."

Within a few moments, everyone disappeared. Some men collected the statue in the crate and carried it out. The heraldry and swarm of attendants that had accompanied the prince were all gone, and the room was dark and silent once more.

"Do you think we dare move?" I asked after a few more moments.

"Why would we do that? I was planning to wait and see if another rat was going to surprise you. You are astonishingly athletic, Miss Elizabeth."

"What? Fitzwilliam Darcy, you are—"

"Still euphoric about the recollection of your legs wrapped around my waist? Indeed, I am."

I smacked his shoulder lightly. "If you dare tell anyone about that..."

"Why bother? I have much better things to do with my mouth." He pulled me closer and showed me.

Some while later, breathless and dizzy, he set me back on the floor. I staggered and grabbed his coat. Then I giggled like I'd had too much wine.

"Uhm... shall we... shall we go now?"

He frowned, cast his eyes upward, and shook his head. "I am sure the Prince is still waddling to his carriage. We should..." *kiss* "stay..." *kiss* "hidden..." *deeper kiss* "a little..." *and more kissing* "longer."

My eyes slipped closed, and it was a fine thing that his arms were tight around me. Otherwise, I surely would have oozed to the floor. "Oh, very well," I sighed dreamily. "You are... such a scoundrel."

"You were the one who asked me to steal something for you. I should say you have no business complaining."

I toyed with that one big, scrumptious curl that fell over his brow. "Who is complaining?"

He laughed and let his forehead rest against mine. "I am. You have ruined me, Elizabeth Bennet. It is no good. I cannot go back to my sedate, ordinary life now."

I shook my head. "But we are safe. You switched the statues out, the prince is happy, and no one saw us."

"Oh, dash the stupid statues. I am talking about you, slowly cutting my heart out of my chest and tucking it neatly into your little palm. *You* are the actual thief between the two of us."

I slipped my hands further up his neck to the back of his head, stopping just short of that row of stitches I'd pricked into his scalp the first day we met. "Well, then, Fitzwilliam Darcy. What do you plan to do about it? Put up the hue and cry? Turn me in to the constable?"

"Wash your hands."

I squinted. "What?"

He pushed the front of our crate open and took me by the hand. "Come. You're scratching the devil out of me with that clay all over your hands and arms. What did you do, bathe in the stuff?"

I arched my shoulders and held my chin aloft. "I was improvising. I told you I knew nothing about clay sculpting."

He slipped an arm around my waist. "Then first, we find a bucket where I will enjoy washing every speck of clay from your satiny skin. Then, I mean to take you back to Darcy House and put my great-great grandmother Darcy's enormous sapphire ring right..." He lifted my hand to kiss my fourth finger, grimy and everything... "There. And I hope you will leave it on."

My heart started skipping. He wanted *me*? Forever? I would have laughed and leaped into his arms to kiss him senseless, but it was more fun to tease him. I forced a contemplative sniff, regarded my hand, and frowned. "I'll have to see if it fits."

"Oh, I'll make sure it fits," he said in a husky voice.

And then he dipped me backward for a kiss to make all our other indiscretions pale by comparison. So, *that* was what a man's tongue felt like, dancing with my own. And oh, my gracious, but how did he have enough hands to make me feel them *everywhere?*

I could get used to that.

"What do you say, Elizabeth Bennet? Care to give up your life of crime?"

I laughed and wrapped his cravat around my fist to make him keep kissing me. I think I ruined it, but he could probably afford another one. "If you insist."

Darcy

RICHARD WAS STILL AT my townhouse when Elizabeth and I returned. And with him, of course, was George Wickham, who looked to have consumed half a dozen bottles from my cellar. That was probably Richard's way of preventing Wickham from palming the silverware—keep him sedated. Richard shot to his feet, and Wickham saluted groggily when we walked into the drawing room.

"Miss Elizabeth Bennet of Longbourn, may I present my cousin, Colonel Fitzwilliam?" I said.

The stupid grin Richard got on his face... I swear, the man loves it when he feels he has discovered my secrets. The whiff of a suspicion that I had fallen for some Hertfordshire lady had nearly driven him to distraction for the last few days. He bowed gallantly over Elizabeth's hand. "I am delighted to make your acquaintance, Miss Bennet."

When Richard straightened and shot me a smug look, I met his gaze and flicked my head toward Wickham, who was still clambering to his feet. Richard nodded in understanding. "Ah, Miss Bennet, has Darcy ever told you about the magnificent library he has?"

Elizabeth laughed. "Colonel, there are many things I am still learning about Mr. Darcy."

"Well, come! Let me show you one of them. You don't mind, old boy, do you?" He turned back to Elizabeth and firmly attached her hand to his forearm. "He doesn't mind. Darcy is ridiculously proud of his library and secretly delights when someone else shows it off for him. Away with us, Miss Bennet!"

Elizabeth chuckled and gave me that arch look of hers as Richard led her out of the room.

"Just be careful not to be *too* charming, Richard," I called as they passed through the door. "I am hoping she will still want to marry me after meeting you."

Richard guffawed and patted her hand just before they disappeared into the hall. "I knew it! Oh, Miss Bennet, we are going to be fine friends."

I sighed and turned my attention back to George Wickham. He had given up the attempt at standing and was merely grinning at me from the sofa. With a glass of expensive claret in his hand. "Cheers, Darcy." Only it came out sounding like, "Sheeres, dasheee."

I examined my pocket watch, then put it away. "How was your journey into Kent?"

"Devilish brutal," he slurred. "Why did old Richard drive us back through the night?" He hiccoughed. "Could've been..." Another hiccough. "Highwaymen."

"I pity the highwayman who takes on Colonel Fitzwilliam's carriage." I eased myself into a chair, as it was apparent that Wickham would not be any good at standing just now. "And it was a matter that required haste."

Wickham tipped his glass up, but it was already empty. With a sigh, he put it down. "Suppose now that you're back, it's no good asking for another bottle."

I shook my head.

"So, what was that all about, Darcy? Aren't you too saintly to soil your hands by employing me to burgle some statue from Lady Catherine?" He hiccoughed again.

"As it happens, Lady Catherine was the thief, robbing a man in significant straits of the money he was counting on to keep a roof over his head. I will see that the true owner is now paid in full. Not to worry, Wickham. I will be certain that Lady Catherine is happy, and that all is fair."

Wickham grunted and rubbed his eyes. "Who made you the arbiter over us all?"

I shook my head. "Someone who asked for my help. And thank goodness my task is at an end." I withdrew a fifty-pound note from my breast pocket. "This should be sufficient for your troubles."

That got him to his feet. He tossed a lazy salute and grinned like a lush. "Anytime you need something stolen, Darcy, I'm your man."

"That will not be happening. This was far too close to the edge of morality for me."

Wickham shrugged and started for the hall, but then he rounded on me with a sloppy grin. "By the by, how is your dear sister? She must be nearly grown by now."

I pointed at the door. "Out."

He grumbled and turned away. And that was the last I ever saw of George Wickham: the man who taught me to pick locks.

E LIZABETH DIDN'T EVEN HEAR me when I slipped into the library behind her. Richard was showing her where to find certain categories of books, for I had a precise system of organization on my shelves. She was still wandering with her mouth open and her eyes scanning from floor to ceiling, but Richard slipped out when he saw me.

I didn't interrupt Elizabeth's wanderings. It was too delicious to see her here, in my home, for the first time. I merely leaned against the fireplace mantel and watched her—the quiet way she moved about the room, her light steps, the grace of her form. Yes, my life with Elizabeth at my side would take on a new brilliance. Once, there was a time when I would have objected to the small fortune that would come with her or her lack of connections. Now, I knew beyond a doubt that what Elizabeth did have was what my soul thirsted for the most. She was laughter and light and the one person who could challenge me to reach beyond myself. I needed her like I needed air.

But more than anything, I longed to be the one she always turned to for help. I wanted to be the man she trusted to comfort her, to protect her, and to make things right for her. I wanted to be the one who got to show his adoration every day, to be the lucky man who got to hold her to his heart and make her laugh, and maybe even do something crazy with her when the mood struck us.

She rounded the corner, walking almost sideways as she took in all the books on the shelves, and still, she had not seen me. And that gave me a rather impish notion. Lightly, I slipped behind her, then as she took her next slow step, I scooped her into my arms and dipped her backward over my bent knee for a kiss.

Note: Elizabeth does not react well when startled. I now have a black eye, and I am quite proud of it.

"William! Oh, are you all right? I did not mean to…"

I put my hand up. "No, no, that was my fault. I ought to know better by now. Help me up off the floor, will you?"

Pearly teeth sank into her lip as she grabbed my hand with both of hers to tug me to my feet. She wasn't much help, really—I am, after all, approximately twice her size. But I loved that she didn't shrink from the challenge, all the same. I stood on my own, still clinging to her hand long after I was on my feet.

Her expression had grown suspicious. "What are you doing now, William?"

I put my other hand into my pocket and withdrew a sparkling sapphire ring. "I believe I told you earlier. Shall we see if it fits?"

She blushed and looked down, spreading her fingers so I could choose the one I liked best to slip the gold ring on. Her gaze slid to me as she held it up to the light for examination. "Are you sure? It seems I have a fearful habit of injuring you."

"Yes, but you're getting better at it. I think with a little more practice, you could be a true proficient."

"Cheeky rascal! For that, I shall have to invent some form of penance."

I drew her into my arms, relishing how she let her body mold to mine. Her hands slid up my chest, then snaked into my hair, and she even hooked one foot behind my leg, creating… interesting sensations. That time hiding together in the crate had gone to good use. "And what is that?"

Elizabeth got a wicked grin and leaned close to whisper against my lips. "You will have to take me back to Hertfordshire and explain all this to my family. My mother will want to know why I am wearing a boulder on my finger, and my father will be curious about what happened to his sculpture."

I laughed weakly. "One day at a time, love. Let's do that..." I kissed her "...tomorrow."

Elizabeth shrugged. "Very well. I suppose until then, I will just..."

That was an excellent idea.

EPILOGUE

Elizabeth

T HE DRAWING ROOM AT Netherfield Park looked a great deal better with all the furnishings uncovered and the candles lit.

Ten days had passed since our little adventure in London. Mr. Bingley was now fully in residence, having met all the neighbors and selected his favorite—already. No one was surprised when he took to calling on Jane nearly every day, and Mama was already making wedding preparations in anticipation of my sister snagging the most eligible bachelor in Hertfordshire.

But today was about William and me.

Though a betrothal dinner ought typically to be hosted by the bride's family, Mr. Bingley had graciously opened his new home to nearly everyone within fifty miles. It was a fortunate thing, too, because everyone seemed inclined to accept the invitation—including the Earl of Matlock, who looked curiously like that sketch I was supposed to turn into a clay bust.

With him came Lady Matlock, Colonel Fitzwilliam, and two or three others whose rank had impressed Mr. Bingley's sisters into civility and Mama into silence. Aunt and Uncle Gardiner had even made the journey from London, so we could not have all fit in Longbourn's drawing room.

Charlotte found me after supper when we ladies had all withdrawn from the dining room. She settled beside me with a cup of coffee and an exceedingly smug grin. "Well, Lizzy? How well do you like the business of being betrothed?"

I smiled and lowered my cup. "What is that supposed to mean?"

"Hypocrite! You know very well what it means. Does your Mr. Darcy kiss better than that burglar who was besieging our neighborhood?"

I lifted a shoulder. "Yes, and no."

Her eyebrows shot up. "Well, is it yes, or is it no?"

"I believe I shall demur by observing that Mr. Darcy improves upon closer acquaintance."

Charlotte pursed her lips, then shook her head. "You are not telling me something, but you may keep your little secret. Would you like to know mine?"

"Oh, by all means." I sipped from my coffee and waited.

She preened and straightened. "Do you recall how I swore that Mr. Collins only wanted instruction in the art?"

I almost spilled coffee on my skirt. "No. Charlotte, you didn't!"

"I very much *did*, and I have never been so correct about anything in my life. You have no idea what you missed out on."

I set my cup aside, for my stomach had suddenly died. I clutched it and tried with all my might not to gag. "Charlotte, you cannot be serious."

"I most certainly am. Honestly, when you get past the tea slurping and the excessive sweating, he really is quite a catch."

I winced. "And the complete and utter obsequious arrogance, and the long hair he combs over his bald spot."

"Oh, I talked him into cutting that off. He likes it when I stroke his head."

My eyes crossed. "Charlotte, I'm going to be sick. Can you please—"

"We are to be married, you know. He wrote to me once he returned to Rosings with Lady Catherine's approval. Fancy that! Me, married at twenty-seven!"

I tried to swallow and started fanning myself. "He had to ask Lady Catherine if he could marry you?"

"Yes, I was so honored! By the by, did you know that Lady Catherine had a burglar herself?"

A hint of a smile tugged at my mouth, but I fought it back. "How very interesting."

"Indeed! The thief took only an old statue. No money, no jewelry. Is that not odd?"

"Mmm-hmm." I hid behind my coffee cup. "Very odd."

"Yes, but stranger still is what happened after. Lady Catherine has a daughter, you know."

"Anne de Bourgh—yes, I have heard of her. There was once a rumor that she was to marry my Mr. Darcy, but there was nothing in it."

"Hah! A fine thing she did not because she had an 'encounter' with the thief on his way out. And do you know, it sounds very much like the same troublemaker we had here a fortnight ago because they say he kissed her so soundly that she forgot her own name for half an hour afterward. There, does that not sound like the same blighter who was here for a time?"

It was all I could do not to burst into a most unladylike belly laugh. "Indeed, it does!"

"And they say," Charlotte continued, "that Lady Catherine has posted a reward to find the man."

"Why? Because he stole her statue?"

Charlotte shrugged. "My theory is that he stole Anne de Bourgh's heart. Pity for her. I am sure he is off merrily robbing and kissing elsewhere."

"Well, I have it on good authority that he is not, but I cannot reveal how I know that. Ah, has Mr. Collins said anything about Lady Catherine's statue?"

"Sadly gone forever. But she is not mourning, not since she bought another. I did not hear where she got it or what she paid, but she is terribly enamored of it."

"Oh?"

"Indeed, for she had it inspected, and everyone believes it is a genuine Michelangelo!"

I blinked. "A... a Michelangelo?"

"Yes, is that not something?"

I hadn't swallowed my last gulp of coffee, and I almost choked on it. "Ah... indeed." I stared blankly across the room. "Charlotte, are you certain?"

"That is what Mr. Collins said. Lady Catherine is pleased as punch. I daresay she hardly misses the other one."

I coughed.

"Why, Lizzy, are you all right? Shall I get you some cake? More coffee?"

I shook my head. "No, Charlotte, I am perfectly well. But if you will excuse me, I see the gentlemen are coming to join us, and there is something I must ask Mr. Darcy."

"Very well. He is a fine specimen, Lizzy. I only hope he is half as romantic as Mr. Collins when you are alone."

I tasted bile. "Ah... yes. Well, good for you, Charlotte. Excuse me, please."

Darcy

E LIZABETH WAS RADIANT THIS evening. I had that thought at least five times as I crossed the room with my after-dinner coffee. Her head was bowed in conversation with Miss Lucas, and she probably did not know I was staring at her.

It was difficult not to. Something about her drew my eye more powerfully than any art I had ever beheld. She was the center of my universe, my exquisite Venus, my bold Athena, and I was merely the awestruck admirer.

I probably looked like a fool whenever I was around her—Richard teased me freely about it, and even the earl had made one or two comments about me losing my touch at slipping nooses. But who cares about a bit of ribbing when the masterpiece herself becomes his? A man is permitted to drool a bit over his bride.

I wandered to the fireplace mantel, leaning my elbow on the ledge and contenting myself with watching her. How strange that this was the very spot where I had first set eyes on her!

"Well, well, Mr. Darcy," said a voice beside me. "I trust all your business in London is come to a satisfactory conclusion."

I tore my gaze from Elizabeth and turned to her father. "Indeed, it is."

"And... His Highness was... pleased?"

I chuckled softly. "I believe you received what was owed you, did you not?"

"Well, as to that, I had thought it would be somewhat more. There was mention of... well, you saw the letter as well, no doubt."

I set my cup aside. "That was on the assumption that the sculpture was what you represented it to be. But it was not, was it?"

Mr. Bennet squinted as if he did not understand, so I gestured to the four vases gracing the mantel. "Do you know, it is odd, these antiquities. So difficult to know precisely what one is looking at. I suppose that is often the case, that a counterfeit is sold for a genuine artifact, with no one the wiser."

My future father-in-law laughed and shook his finger at me. "Ah, I see what you are about, Mr. Darcy. Well, come out with it."

"I do not need to. I believe we understand each other, and I trust there will be no more 'ancient works of art' brokered by the unsuspecting Mr. Gardiner. And as for the rest of what was promised, it has been safely delivered to a man who *did* sell a genuine artifact to the prince. All is as it should be."

Bennet sighed. "Well, have it your way. You young people have no imagination anymore."

Elizabeth chose that instant to rise from the sofa and walk toward us, and my heart began cavorting in my chest. How did she always do that to me? "I must protest that accusation," I told Mr. Bennet. "My imagination at this moment is rather vivid, and if you will pardon me, I mean to let it have a bit of rein." I bowed slightly and met Elizabeth halfway across the room.

She set her hand on my arm. "William, you will never believe what Charlotte has just told me!"

"I am certain I will not, but should we not discuss it privately?"

"Oh! Oh, yes, I think that would be best. But where can we go? The house is full."

I thought for a moment. "I have an idea." I escorted her from the drawing room to the outer hall and then toward the service corridor. No one was about, and I opened the door to a closet under the stairwell. "Quickly. Shh."

Elizabeth gave me that coy, hesitant look of hers, then shrugged and ducked inside the closet. A moment later, I joined her and closed the door. A broom fell against my back, and I kicked a mop bucket when I tried to dodge. It was only by fumbling against Elizabeth that I kept from banging my head on the low ceiling.

She pulled me to her, grabbing the front of my jacket and waltzing me about, so I stood under the tallest part of our little hiding place. "Why did you think of coming here? I thought you were claustrophobic."

"I'm cured." I cupped her cheek, letting my fingers drift into her hair, and lost myself. She tasted like spices and honey, and her lips felt like buttery velvet against my skin. But the best part was the way her breath faltered and caught whenever I kissed her a little more deeply or feathered my tongue down her chin to nibble her throat.

"William," she gasped after several minutes, "I didn't ask to see you privately so you could steal a kiss."

"I think I have stolen several by now," I murmured against her ear.

She shivered and laughed. "Quite so. But Charlotte says that sculpture... ooh, I like that."

"I can tell." I kissed down the nape of her neck. "More?"

"No, no, please. Be serious for just a moment."

I sighed and left off kissing her. "Very well. What is it?"

"Charlotte says that Lady Catherine's expert told her that the Eros sculpture is a genuine Michelangelo! Is that possible?"

"Oh, Michelangelo, my foot. The thing is cut from English marble if I ever saw it."

I couldn't see her face, but I could imagine that delicious crease between her brows when she was deep in thought. "So... it *is* a fake?"

"My darling, I have come to agree with your father in this one thing, at least. The Eros sculpture is some of the finest craftsmanship it has ever been my pleasure to behold. Regardless of its pedigree, it is a genuine masterpiece. I am certain that Lady Catherine is proud to own it."

I bent down to kiss her again—for that was *my* idea of a productive hiding session under the stairs—but she pushed me back. "But... but..."

"Let it go, my love. As with people, I care less about where it comes from than I do the quality of the individual. Our duty is not to go around telling everyone else about their possessions. Let us enjoy our own, instead."

Her arms snaked around my neck, and she pulled me closer. "And what are those?"

"Well, I..." I stroked down her bare arm with the tips of my fingers, proud of the gooseflesh I made. "I just acquired the fairest, most magnificent work of art anyone in England has ever set eyes on."

"Oh, did you?"

"Indeed."

"And how did you find this work of art?"

"Now, that is a secret I must keep to myself."

Elizabeth toyed with a hank of my hair, twirling it around her finger and making me weak in the knees. "And why is that, you rogue?"

I leaned down and caressed her ear with my lips. "Because I stole her."

KEEP READING MORE OF Darcy and Elizabeth's romantic hijinks in *Along for the Ride* by Alix James or *London Holiday* by Nicole Clarkston!

From Alix

T HANK YOU FOR INDULGING with me and spending a little time with Darcy and Elizabeth.

I hope you've had a delightful escape to Pemberley. I'd love it if you would share this family with your friends so they can experience a love to last for the ages. As with all my books, I have enabled lending to make it easier to share. If you leave a review for *Mr. Darcy Steal a Kiss* on Amazon, Goodreads, Book Bub or your own blog, I would love to read it! Email me the link at **NClarkston35@gmail.com.**

Would you like to read more of Darcy and Elizabeth's romance? I have a fun one for you to try next! Dive into *Along for the Ride* by Alix James or *London Holiday* by my alternate pen name, Nicole Clarkston. Laugh along with our favorite couple as they find the love they were destined for!

And if you're hungry for more, including a free ebook of satisfying short tales, stay up to date on upcoming releases and sales by joining my newsletter: https://dashboard.mailerlite.com/forms/249660/7 3866370936211000/share

Also By Alix James

The Short and Sassy Series:

Unintended

Spirited Away

Indisposed

Love and Other Machines

Elizabeth Bennet: Short and Sassy Compilation

The Sweet Sentiments Series:

When the Sun Sleeps

Cuando el Sol se Duerm (Spanish Translation)

Queen of Winter

Reina del Invierno (Spanish Translation)

A Fine Mind

Una Mente Noble (Spanish translation)

The Frolic and Romance Series:

A Proper Introduction

A Good Memory is Unpardonable

Along for the Ride

The Mr. Darcy Series:

Mr. Darcy Steals a Kiss

Also By Nicole Clarkston

Pride and Prejudice Variations

Tempted

The Rogue's Widow

Nefarious

London Holiday

These Dreams

The Courtship of Edward Gardiner

Rumours and Recklessness

North and South Variations

Nowhere but North

Northern Rain

No Such Thing as Luck

Anthologies

Rational Creatures

Falling for Mr Thornton

Spanish Translations

Rumores e Imprudencias

Vacaciones en Londres

Nefasto

Italian Translations

Una Vacanza a Londra

FREE EBOOK FROM NICOLE!

Sign up for Nicole Clarkston's newsletter and receive a free ebook of shorts and vignettes.

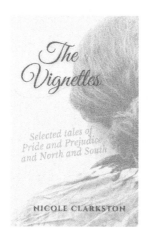